"It's way too gross to have to watch my own mother hanging all over some guy."

With that comment, Meghan left the room in a huff.

Libby closed her eyes and drew in a breath designed to calm her. It didn't work. Neither did her fervent prayer that when she opened her eyes again, Hal would have somehow magically disappeared.

He was still there.

"If what I did might be construed in any way, shape or form as hanging all over you, I hope you'll forgive me. I didn't mean—"

He laughed.

"You think that was funny?"

Shaking his head, Hal stood. "I think you're way too serious."

"What am I being too serious about?"

"Look," he said, "I don't want you to get the wrong idea, but I'm a single guy. And my hand might be hurt, and I might be going stir-crazy from being cooped up at home, but I'm far from dead. So the whole thing about you hanging all over me…" A smile tickled the corners of his mouth.

"Your daughter was overreacting," he said. "She was imagining things. You were not out of line. You were not hanging all over me. But—" with a wink, he walked out the door "—it's a pretty interesting thought."

Connie Lane

remembers when she got her first library card and the first book she took out of the Cleveland Public Library: *Horton Hatches the Egg*. That was the official start of her love of reading; writing stories naturally followed. She majored in English at Cleveland State University, studied literature at Queen's College, Oxford University, England, and turned her love of words and her overactive imagination into a career in journalism and corporate communications. After the births of her two children, she began writing fiction and has published nearly thirty books. In addition to category romance, she's written single-title and historical romance as well as mysteries, and has taught writing to aspiring novelists. She has been nominated for a RITA® Award by Romance Writers of America. She lives in northeast Ohio with her family and Oscar, a rescued Jack Russell, and Ernie, an adorable Airedale puppy.

Knit Two Together

CONNIE LANE

KNIT TWO TOGETHER

copyright © 2007 by Connie Laux

isbn-13: 978-0-373-88130-7

isbn-10: 0-373-88130-4

TheNextNovel.com

 HARLEQUIN®

PRINTED IN U.S.A.

From the Author

Dear Reader,

If you've ever walked into a knitting shop and been blown away by the colors, the textures and the possibilities of what you could do with all that yarn, then we've got a lot in common!

You see, like millions of others, I'm addicted to knitting. (And to crochet and weaving, too.) I daydream about the possibilities of what might happen when needles, yarn and a bit of imagination come together. That's what I was thinking about when I first came up with the idea for *Knit Two Together*.

Like all novels, this one started as nothing more than that rough idea. All of it came together there in Metropolitan Knits, a fictional version of what I think of as the ideal yarn shop. Libby learns to take her experiences there and knit them into the fabric of her family's life, seamlessly blending past and present and carrying on traditions that, like knitting, give continuity and form to our world.

Happy knitting!

Connie Lane
P.S.—I love to hear from my readers. You can contact me at conmielane@earthlink.net.

How many people can one book be dedicated to?
This one is for Diane, Emilie, Jasmine and Karen
with thanks and appreciation.

It's also for Cheryl I, Susan, Cheryl II and Patty,
the great staff at Soft 'n Sassy—the world's best
yarn shop—in Broadview Heights, Ohio.

And for Georgia, Eleanor, Carol, Ruth, Pat, Karin, Gail
and all the other talented knitters I've met through the
years. Thank you for many hours of companionship,
advice and inspiration.

CHAPTER 1

"Of course I want to sell the yarn shop. It's just that—"

Libby Cartwright would have liked to continue her phone conversation, but at that moment she noticed a man standing outside her office door. He was holding a clipboard that contained an official-looking form, and something told her she was going to need two free hands, so she mumbled an excuse to the real-estate agent on the other end of the line. She propped the phone between her ear and her shoulder and motioned for the man to come in. She accepted the clipboard and pen he handed her, and when she scrawled her name and the title Office Manager on the line above where it read *Responsible party*, her hands didn't even tremble. At least not too much.

While the man tore off one sheet of the form she'd just signed, dropped it on her desk and backed out of her office, she returned to her conversation.

"I told you, Mr. Harper, getting rid of the knitting shop has been priority number one ever since I found out about the inheritance." The noise of a scrape and bump from out in the hallway attracted her attention, and Libby glanced out her door to where two men struggled to haul away the just-delivered printer/fax/copier she had ordered three months earlier. With everything else that was happening at Cartwright, Remington and Hawes, no one in the office had even had a chance to read the how-to manual, much less learn to operate the behemoth.

The equipment was unused. Practically untouched. And far easier to return because of it.

"I hear what you're saying, Mrs. Cartwright." The sound of Will Harper's voice drew Libby's attention away from the commotion in the hallway. "But what you're saying and what you're doing sound like two different things to me."

"What I'm saying is that I want to sell the yarn shop. What I'm doing..."

Libby drummed her fingers against the windowsill. What she was doing was hesitating, plain and simple.

She twitched her shoulders to get rid of the thought, scolding herself as she did. By now she should have known better—there were some things she couldn't so easily shake.

"I have no intention of ever reopening the shop," she told Will and reminded herself. "I don't want to run it. For one thing, the shop is in Cleveland and I live in Pittsburgh."

"Which is exactly why you should be up on your desk doing the happy dance right about now." She heard the click of his cigarette lighter and his quick intake of breath. "Tip-Top is all over the West and they claim they're going to own the drugstore market in Ohio, too, in just a few years. Lucky for you, they want to start in Cleveland and they're not looking for some pristine parcel out in the burbs. They want an established neighborhood and they're willing to raze a city block to build one of their stores. Your mother's property isn't the only one they're looking at, remember. We need to jump on this as quickly as we can. The offer they're making…well, honestly, as I told you before, I don't think you'll ever do any better."

"They're lowballing me."

Were they? Libby wasn't sure. In the two years since she'd taken over the job of office manager for the law firm, she'd discovered that she was a whiz at scheduling, a crackerjack manager of people and something of a genius when it came to finding the best prices on supplies and equipment. But real estate was a whole new ball game. Still, talking money seemed like the appropriate thing to do at this stage. As for balking at the price, wasn't that what real-estate deals were all about? Besides, it was a plausible excuse for her hesitation. And a better comeback than the truth.

The knit shop is the only thing I have—the only thing I've ever had—from my mother. Once I sell, it means I'm severing this one last tie and quitting. For good. Forever.

"Mrs. Cartwright? Don't you agree?"

Libby snapped out of her thoughts. "I'm sorry. This connection isn't all that good," she said, because it was better than admitting she hadn't been listening. "You were saying—"

"That I'll bet the money from this deal would come in handy right about now. For you and for your husband."

As if Will could see her, Libby looked at the receiver in wonder. "How do you know about Rick?"

"Hey, I know the economy stinks. I'll bet it's hit you folks hard."

Hard was putting it mildly.

Libby dropped into the chair behind her desk, and though she didn't know how, she sensed that Will was reading her mind.

"A big influx of cash might help out, right?" he asked. "Am I onto something here?"

He was. Libby could take the cash from the sale of Barb's Knits and dump it right into the firm's account. It wasn't a magic bullet, but it would help staunch the sea of red ink.

Sending back the mother of all printer/fax/copiers was just the tip of the iceberg. There were staff cuts yet to be made and that meant employees—friends—would spend the summer, the worst job-hunting time of the year, pounding the pavement.

"So…" Will eased back into the subject. "You climbing up on that desk of yours? Is that why you're so quiet? Should I put on the music so you can start dancing?"

Libby managed a weak smile. "Not yet. Maybe if I just—" She caught herself before the words slipped out.

Maybe if I just went to Cleveland and looked at the shop.

So many times in the past months she'd suggested it. And

every time Rick had reminded her the trip was a complete waste of time and inconvenient as well. After all, she had the firm to worry about, as well as their daughter Meghan's schedule. Going to Cleveland to see a shop that didn't mean anything to her and that had been left her by a woman she hadn't seen in years...Why take the chance of reopening wounds that had taken so long to heal?

Face it, Lib. Inside her head, Rick's familiar words were a mantra. *That rift is too wide ever to cross.*

She told herself not to forget it, reminded herself that the past was gone and nothing could change it and got down to business.

"Maybe if Tip-Top ups their offer," she told Will.

He chuckled. "Even a miracle worker like me couldn't pull off that one. They've seen the property, you haven't. Maybe you'd feel better about the whole thing if you came to Cleveland and—"

"No." Libby answered quickly and refused to reconsider. "But I could use more money. I thought the property would be worth more. It's the retail space on the first floor and the apartment upstairs, right? That's like getting two properties."

"Tip-Top doesn't give a damn about square footage. They're going to knock the place down! Believe me, this offer is a gift. And, remember, if we play hard to get, they've got their eye on a second spot across town. What do you say? It would be one less thing on your plate. A weight off your shoulders. An albatross from around your neck. A—"

"Okay, all right!" Libby had to laugh. There was nothing as over-the-top as a Realtor anxious to seal a deal. "I know it's the right thing to do. And it would really help us out."

It wasn't an outright surrender, but it was pretty close. "You'll talk to your husband?" Will asked.

"I'll talk to my husband," she promised. "But you know the final decision is mine."

"And I know you'll make the right one. How about if I tell Tip-Top we'll have an answer for them this afternoon?"

"That seems awfully quick. How about tomorrow? Or—"

"They'll go somewhere else."

"Yes. Of course." Libby's breath was tight in her throat. "This afternoon," she said. "I'll talk to you then."

"And we'll put this deal to bed. You'll be glad when it's over, Mrs. Cartwright."

She had no doubt of it. It was getting there that was, unexplainably, the painful part.

Libby hung up. She'd told Will she'd run the Tip-Top offer by Rick, but she really didn't have to. She knew what he would say.

She'd talk to Rick anyway. It was how partnerships worked—how their marriage had always worked and one of the reasons that, after sixteen years, theirs was as strong as ever.

She was set to leave her office when she grabbed the file folder that contained her thoughts on staff cuts. As long as she was going to have Rick's undivided attention, she might as well get as much business accomplished as possible.

The door to Rick's office wasn't closed, but Libby rapped it with her knuckles anyway. She'd already stepped inside when she saw that he was on the phone, so while he finished she toed the threshold.

She didn't mind waiting. It gave her the perfect excuse to step back and look at her husband.

At forty, Rick still made her heart skip a beat, and watching him, a smile tugged at the corners of her mouth. As always, he was impeccably dressed in a charcoal suit that was a perfect complement for his slim runner's body. His dark hair was touched with gray, and she suspected that over the next years he'd turn into a carbon copy of his handsome, silver-haired father. Rick's eyes were blue, and as he talked, the little dimple in his left cheek made a showing. She remembered that when they'd met in law school, that dimple was the first thing she'd noticed about him. That and the fact that she'd instantly fallen head over heels in love with him.

All these years later, nothing had changed. Oh, they'd had their rough patches—didn't all couples?—but they'd come through stronger and happier. Life was good even if it wasn't perfect.

Even if Rick insisted she sell Barb's Knits without once taking a look at it and maybe getting some insight into the mystery that was her mother's life.

The thought hit Libby out of the blue, and with a shake of her shoulders she got rid of it.

Logic, she reminded herself, was more important than emotion. Besides, any emotion she might have felt for Barb had evaporated years before.

Rick motioned to Libby that he'd be right with her.

"You're sure?" he said into the phone. "Yeah. Of course. You know that's true. I just didn't think—" He spun his chair toward the window. "I'll take care of it," he said. "Don't worry. We'll just need to move on this faster and hey, that's not such a bad thing, is it?"

As soon as he hung up, Libby stepped into the office. "Problems?"

Rick turned his chair around. "Nothing I can't handle." He looked her over, and for the second time in as many minutes, Libby felt her heart skip a beat. She swore she could feel a little lick of fire every time Rick looked at her.

This time, though, his gaze stopped at the file folder she carried.

"You want to talk business."

Libby dropped into the guest chair across from where Rick sat. "Is that so unusual?"

"No, it's just that…" He cleared his throat. "I've got some things to talk to you about, too."

"Oh, no, buster. Me first. You're not stealing my thunder." For reasons she'd already examined and dismissed as unfounded, she wasn't as excited about selling the knit shop as she knew Rick would be. But she didn't mind pretending. After all the stress caused by the business slump the law firm was experiencing, he deserved a little pampering. "Good news. I got an offer on the property in Cleveland."

"Take it."

"Just like that? You don't want to know how much they offered?"

He shrugged. "I don't much care."

"I thought you did. I thought—"

"You're always putting words in my mouth." Rick got up and crossed the room to close his office door. He stood with his back to her. "You know I didn't mean that the way it sounded. I'm just thinking about you, Lib. You need to have that Palmer woman out of your life."

"That Palmer woman…" Libby gave the words the same inflection Rick had. As if they tasted bad. "She was my mother."

"And a lousy one at that."

"There's no denying it. But that doesn't mean—"

"What? That you should go on some kind of Indiana Jones quest?" Rick spun around. "You're thinking about going to Cleveland again, aren't you? Let's face it, you're not going to find something there that explains why Barb treated you the way she did. Or why, after all these years, she left you her business. What are you looking for, a letter? 'Dear Libby, here are all the reasons I abandoned you, now you can live happily ever after'?"

"Of course not!" Though she denied it, Libby had to admit—at least to herself—that the thought had occurred to her. It was preposterous, sure. That didn't make it any less appealing. And Rick should have known that.

She pulled in a breath to steady her racing heart. "I didn't come in here to argue," she said. "We've talked about it all before."

"Ad nauseam."

"Really?" Tears stung Libby's eyes. She sniffed and stood. "And here I thought we were discussing an important part of my life because you cared about me."

In an instant Rick's anger dissolved. He stepped toward her but stopped short of folding her into a hug. "Of course I care," he said. "I'm sorry. I've just been so preoccupied. You know that, Lib. You know I've got other things on my mind. That's why when you said you had an offer, I figured we'd put an end to this whole thing."

If he wasn't going to make the first move, Libby would. She reached for Rick's hand and folded her fingers over his. "It's just that now that it's come down to crunch time—"

"Nobody's better in a crisis than you are." He flashed a smile that disappeared quickly. "You know this is the right thing to do, Lib. It's time to put that part of your life to rest."

"I know. I have, but—"

"We could really use the money."

"Yeah." Libby pulled in a breath and let it out slowly. "You're right."

Rick untangled himself from her grasp and retreated to the other side of his desk. "One more thing off our to-do list."

"But there are other things we need to discuss." She waved the file folder. "I've been going over the list of people we could let go."

"You know we have to do it."

"I know. But I've been thinking…we could keep three clerical people. If we cut somebody with a higher salary."

Rick dropped into his chair. "I was thinking the same thing."

Libby was relieved. She flipped open the folder, took out the paperwork on Belinda Acton, the firm's newest attorney, and handed it to Rick. "She's been here only a few months," she said. "There aren't any strong ties and she's not responsible for many billable hours. Besides, she'll find something else fast."

Rick's gaze snapped to her. "It's out of the question."

"But that's crazy, Rick. Belinda will be sitting pretty in a matter of weeks."

"She stays."

"Then who?"

He pulled in a breath, but his gaze never wavered from hers. "You."

Libby opened her mouth to respond, but the words refused to form on her lips.

"Come on, Lib, it's the most plausible plan and you know it. You're going to quit anyway."

She heard what Rick was saying, but it was as if he was speaking another language. Her knees turned to jelly, and

Libby dropped into the closest chair. "I have no plans to quit. I never did. I took this job when you needed extra help. I've been good for the firm."

"And you've got the place running like clockwork. I'm grateful. But, come on, let's be honest. You also know that you've got something of a pattern. You know, a reputation?"

He smiled at her the way she'd seen him smile at Meghan when their daughter didn't understand her math homework. As if the truth was staring her right in the face and if she looked a little harder she was bound to see it.

"You quit law school," he said.

"Ancient history." It was, and so ridiculous Libby nearly laughed. Until she realized that Rick wasn't kidding. "I quit law school because of you," she said, reminding him though she shouldn't have had to. "We both couldn't afford to stay in school. And let's face it, we all say it isn't real, but that glass ceiling does exist. We knew your income would outpace mine eventually. Besides, I wouldn't have had to quit if your father had paid for your schooling. If you two hadn't been going at each other like cats and dogs—"

"We wouldn't have been going at each other like cats and dogs if I hadn't been dating you. I gave up—"

"What?" Libby rose and looked around the office with its to-die-for view and expensive furnishing. "Looks like you and Daddy kissed and made up."

"Yeah, but not until I had a degree. One I paid for myself."

"You mean one I paid for. I gave up my dream of being an attorney. For you."

"You quit."

As if he'd slapped her, Libby stepped back, but before she could argue, Rick continued. "You quit your book discussion group."

"Oh, come on, that's not even in the same ballpark. Besides, that was because I took the job here!"

"You quit your yoga class."

"When Meghan needed more appointments at the orthodontist."

"You quit everything, Lib. Eventually you'd walk out on the firm, too."

A tear slipped down Libby's cheek. She remembered the phone call he'd been on when she'd walked into his office. "Something's going on. You're not acting like yourself. If it's my idea that we lay off Belinda—"

"Belinda is…" Rick's voice broke. He cleared his throat. "As a matter of fact, that was Belinda on the phone. Belinda and I…well, I know you'll be happy for me. Someday, when you have time to think about it. We've been meaning to tell you, but the time's never been right. And now…" His gaze flickered away. "Belinda and I were planning on getting married anyway, but now…well, we're going to need to accelerate our plans. That's why she called, you see. To tell me she's having my baby."

CHAPTER 2

"All right, you saw it. Can we get out of here now, Mommy? Please!"

At the sound of the pleading voice, Libby jerked to awareness. She looked away from the ramshackle building that had held her attention since she'd gotten out of the car and glanced to her left, where Meghan had a firm hold on the sleeve of her black cotton cardigan.

At fourteen, Meghan was way past calling her "Mommy." Except when she wanted something. The something she wanted now was all too apparent, and as Libby had been doing for the past couple months, she wavered about making a decision as to what to do about it. She had never been the indecisive type before—at least not before Rick caused her world to crumble and her self-esteem to plunge—and the very act of hesitating only made her feel less self-assured. She knew Meghan would pick right up on the weakness and Libby braced herself. No doubt her daughter would be all over her in a second.

"Mommy, come on." Meghan tugged her toward the silver Subaru. "If we leave now, maybe nobody will know we were ever here."

As arguments went, it wasn't the most convincing.

Libby glanced around at the city neighborhood where the buildings stood so close together they might as well have been sided with Velcro. The main street had small businesses interspersed between houses, bars and art galleries. In the few minutes she and Meghan had been standing there staring at the building with the faded sign over the front door that declared it Barb's Knits, they had yet to see one other person come or go at either the bakery on the right or the beauty shop on the left. And, of course, no one was shopping at Barb's Knits these days; the store had been closed for nearly a year.

Always conciliatory, Libby offered her daughter a smile even though she knew it would be met with a sneer. "Honestly, honey, I don't think you have to worry about being seen at the wrong time or in the wrong place. It's early and things are pretty quiet around here. There's not much chance of anybody seeing us. Look over there." She pointed toward a scrappy German shepherd who was eyeballing them from the park across the street. "Looks like he's the welcoming committee, and my guess is he's not going to tell anybody."

"It's creepy." Meghan shivered inside the pink hoodie Libby had bought her at the Gap for her last birthday. "The whole place looks like something out of a Stephen King movie. Look at it!" Her top lip curled, Meghan glanced around the perimeter of the park. For Libby, the old neighborhood had a certain appeal. It was anchored by an imposing church, dotted with park benches, bus stops and coffee houses. Except for Barb's Knits—a little seedier than its neighbors and, surprisingly, a little embarrassing because of it—the surrounding shops had the solid feel that bright, new suburban stores never could. Pride of ownership was reflected in everything from the brightly colored and graphically appealing signs to the window boxes planted with summer annuals. Thinking about the generations of people who had put their blood, sweat and tears into the neighborhood and the new generation that worked just as hard to maintain it, Libby felt a sense of belonging. She was part of that new generation now. She had to live up to the promise of the neighborhood and those who had rescued it from melting into urban decay.

It was a scary thought. And exhilarating, too. None of which meant she didn't sympathize with Meghan.

Like most kids her age, Meghan had been raised to think of the mall as the only place to shop; the bright and the new were all that mattered. Looking back on it now, Libby realized she should have introduced her daughter to the world beyond the confines of their upper-middle-class suburb long before her life—and her marriage—had been pulled out from under her. Whose fault was it that Meghan had seen little of downtown Pittsburgh other than the Science Center, PNC Park, where the Pirates played, and the view from her father's office? This was new territory for Meghan. Not just a new city but a new way of life. A new home. A new beginning.

Just as it was for Libby herself.

With a deep breath for courage, Libby reminded herself that the transition was bound to be frightening. Just as so much of Meghan's life had been these past months since Rick had announced he was filing for divorce.

When Meghan started pleading again, Libby didn't argue. But she wasn't about to give in, either.

"Mommy!" Meghan's voice was anguished. "Come on. Let's get out of here. Let's go home."

"We said we were going to make a go of it, remember?" Libby said, and before her daughter could bring up every argument she'd raised in the six weeks since Libby had decided to come to Cleveland, she held up one hand for silence. "We talked about this, Meghan. We decided it would be a new start. An adventure."

"You decided." Meghan crossed her arms over her chest. It was clearly a case of the proverbial line in the sand, and Libby wasn't in the mood.

"It's the best thing," she reminded her daughter. "For both of us."

"For you, maybe. Not for me. I should be home right now. I should be sitting by the pool at Jennifer's. Or Rollerblading with Emma. Or going to dance class with—"

"There are pools and Rollerblading and dance classes in Cleveland," Libby told her as she'd told her a hundred times before. "You're a great kid. You're popular. You're a good friend. You don't have trouble mixing in and you'd be starting high school back in Cranberry, anyway. Instead of meeting new people there, you'll meet new people here when you start at Central Catholic. You know you will, Meggie. Pretty soon you'll make lots of new friends in Cleveland."

"There's nothing wrong with my old friends."

Libby let out a slow breath. "You're absolutely right. They're great kids and you can e-mail them every day and see them on vacations and on the weekends and holidays when you visit your dad. But here, here is where we're going to start over."

"Daddy's starting over and he didn't have to leave Pittsburgh to do it."

It was a low blow, and just as Meghan had calculated, it slammed into Libby like a fist. She stopped herself from sniping back. Oh, it was tempting, but it wasn't fair to blame Meghan for the pain that gnawed her insides.

"What Daddy's doing is…" Libby almost let her emotions get the best of her. *Immature, selfish* and *just plain boneheaded* were not words she should use to describe Rick. At least not in front of her daughter. Meghan had heard enough of that talk. It was time to turn over a new leaf.

"Daddy's starting over is different," she told Meghan instead and she congratulated herself. If Libby pretended she wasn't talking about the last three months and how her life fell apart and her daughter's world crumbled, she could almost make herself sound logical and objective about the whole thing. "He's got a new wife and he and Belinda are going to have a new baby. We've got each other and—"

"And this trashy place." Meghan turned her back on Barb's Knits. "Did you ever even consider that it might be a dump before you moved us all the way here?"

Of course Libby had. She would have been crazy not to.

But she never imagined it would be this bad.

The thought settled inside her, and even though she knew it wasn't fair, she automatically compared Barb's Knits to the rest of the neighborhood.

The rest of the neighborhood won. Hands down.

Once upon a time—and that must have been a very long time before—the building had been not commercial but residential. It had a stone path that led from the sidewalk where they stood, and on either side of the path, flower beds where dandelions poked out of the soil, reaching for the summer sunshine.

Four steps led to a porch where the paint was chipped and a front door that was so caked with dirt it was hard to tell what color it might once have been. The front window was too dirty to see inside, as were the windows in the apartment above the first-floor retail space.

Home, sweet home.

Libby shook her head, clearing it of the fog of doubt that had settled over her with every mile she put between herself and her old life. She knew better than to be surprised by anything she might find inside or outside the shop. To pretend otherwise would be to admit she was both foolish and naive.

But that didn't mean she thought she hadn't made the right decision by coming to Cleveland.

Libby put on her game face. She wasn't fooling herself and heck, she probably wasn't fooling Meghan either. But maybe if she pretended hard enough, one of these days she'd convince herself it was actually possible to feel alive again.

"It can't hurt to go inside and look around, can it?" Libby asked and—thank goodness—at that moment a man in the park across the street waved to them, and Meghan didn't have a chance to answer. From the look in her eyes to the lower lip thrust out just enough for the world to know she was a martyr and a long-suffering one at that, Libby had no doubt what her daughter would have said.

With a quick look both ways, the man hurried across the street. In one hand he held a red leather leash with an overweight poodle on the end of it. With his other hand he gave Libby the thumbs-up.

"I'm guessing you're the new owner, right? You must be. There hasn't been another person who's taken a look at Barb's old place in as long as I can remember. Unless..." He narrowed his eyes and gave Libby the once-over. "Now that I've opened my mouth, you're not going to tell me you're from the drugstore chain, are you?"

"You sound as if that's not a good thing," Libby said.

The man's expression grew sour. "I guess it's progress, but..."

"But you're not thrilled with the idea of the big-box drugstore taking up most of this block."

"Me and everyone else around here. Well, almost everyone else. Peg over at the beauty shop—" he looked that way "—she says she's not going to budge, but I don't trust her. Barb's Knits sits smack-dab in the center of the block, and the whole entire block is what those Tip-Top folks are after. Everything hinges on the sale of this property, and I'm betting that if Barb's Knits goes, Peg will pull up stakes and go, too. Then there will be nobody stopping those Tip-Top folks. Peg!" He snorted. "She always was one to think of herself first and everyone else dead last. So fess up! You one of them? Or one of us?"

Libby grinned. "One of you. I think. If you're talking about me being the new owner of the property, I am." She introduced herself and shook the man's hand. "And, just so you know, I'm planning on opening the store again. I told the drugstore folks I wasn't interested."

"Hear that, Clyde?" The man bent to rub the dog's head. "That ought to get Peg's knickers in a twist. Told you this nice lady looked like one of the good guys." He stood and smiled at Libby before he hurried along with the dog. "Thanks for not selling to those drugstore creeps."

Watching him go, Libby gave Meghan a playful elbow in the ribs. "See that? We're already superheroes and we just got here. They'll probably change the name of the park in our honor."

"Whatever." Meghan rolled her eyes. Clearly there were things a fourteen-year-old understood that an adult never would.

Reminding herself to cut Meghan some slack, Libby put an arm around her daughter's shoulders. It wasn't as easy as it used to be. Over the past months Meghan had grown at least an inch.

Libby herself wasn't as petite as she was compact and though she struggled to maintain her figure as she was nearing forty, she sometimes looked longingly at Meghan, who was tall and willowy even as she was just entering her teenage years. Libby wondered what it would be like not to have to hem every pair of pants she ever bought.

Meghan's hair was nearly black, her eyes were as blue as sapphires and her complexion was porcelain perfection. They were traits she'd inherited from her father's side of the family and she had yet to learn—thank goodness!—to use them to her best advantage. When she did, Libby knew Meghan would break hearts and—at least until hers was broken in return and she knew how much it hurt—she'd enjoy every minute of it.

Libby, on the other hand, had unremarkable brown hair that tended to curl unless she kept it short and tamed with any number of hair-care products. She liked tailored, classic clothes, traditional styling and lots of color. As long as the colors in question were black, navy-blue, gray or white.

Meghan's growth spurt was just another sign that life was changing. Time was passing, and it was a reminder that Libby couldn't wait for a fairy tale someday to make a new life for herself and her daughter. Today was what they had. It was all that mattered.

"What do you say?" She stepped toward Barb's Knits, taking Meghan along with her. "Should we have a look inside?"

"Do we have to?"

"Unless you want to live out here on the sidewalk."

Beneath her hand, Libby felt her daughter's shoulders rise and fall. "We could go home."

"This is home now."

"We could—"

"Race you to the door." It was a game they hadn't played in years, and Libby couldn't say why she thought of it. She slid her arm from around Meghan's shoulders and hurried up the front steps, fast enough to make it look as if she was willing to compete, but slow enough to allow Meghan to win. It wasn't until she was at the door that she looked back to see Meghan standing exactly where she'd left her.

"You're so embarrassing," Meghan said, and she stomped up to the porch.

"Yeah," Libby said under her breath. "And it worked, didn't it?"

With one hand, she fished in her purse for the key that her mother's attorney had sent. She pulled it out and held it up for Meghan to see.

"You ready?" she asked her daughter.

Am I?

The words taunted Libby. She fingered the key, imagining what she might find on the other side of the door. Was she ready for this glimpse into her mother's life? Libby couldn't lie to herself; she hoped that something on the other side of the door would reveal Barb's character, explain her motives, prove a mother's love she'd never known.

And if she didn't find it?

"Mom!"

Meghan's voice snapped Libby back to reality.

"You gonna go inside or you just gonna stand here and stare?"

Libby tossed the key into the air and caught it. "Gonna go inside," she said and she unlocked the front door. She paused on the threshold, drew in a breath for courage. And immediately gagged.

"I think something's dead in there," she said at the same time Meghan squealed.

Libby wasn't going to let that stop her. She hadn't come hundreds of miles to be chased away by a smell.

There was a wooden chair on the front porch, and Libby propped it against the door to keep it open and allow some air inside.

As ready as she'd ever be, she stepped into Barb's Knits.

"The place is a dump." Meghan was right behind her and as always, she had a way of distilling a situation to its essence.

Barb's Knits was, indeed, a dump.

The room they stepped into must have once been the living room of the first-floor apartment. In addition to a dust-covered counter and cash register on the left, there was a wall of shelves and books directly ahead of them, and across from it, tables where tape measures, scissors and other supplies were piled. Beyond a doorway was another room and from what Libby could see, another past that. She peered through the gloom. There was lots of yarn everywhere, lots of dust and—Libby shivered—even some mouse droppings.

And something else.

In spite of Meghan's half-heard warnings about ghosts, axe murderers and creepy crawlers, Libby started into the next room without hesitation, her attention caught by a display table.

The table had two tiers. The bottom one was stacked with wool, but Libby hardly noticed. Her eyes were on the teddy bear on the top tier. A cocoa-colored bear with one missing eye.

"Mom, you okay?"

"Of course." Libby answered automatically, even though she wasn't sure she was. Though she had no clear memory of the bear, there was something vaguely familiar about it. He was dressed in a fisherman knit sweater—handmade by the looks of it—and the fur on his right arm was nearly gone as if years of hugs had worn it away. Instinctively Libby touched the bear with one finger, then stepped back. She swore he was watching her with that one good eye of his.

"Mom!" Meghan's voice called from the front room. "You're awfully quiet in there. Did you get kidnapped?"

"I'm just looking around," she told Meghan. "That's all."

"Yeah, right. And I just fell off a turnip truck."

It was what Libby always said when Meghan tried to pull a fast one on her. Libby smiled grimly.

Meghan stepped through the wide arched doorway that separated what had once been the living room from the dining room, caught sight of the bear and hurried over to scoop it into her arms. "Hey, he's actually kind of cute. And, look, he's wearing a little sweater! It doesn't look nasty and dirty like some of this other stuff around here, does it?"

"Put him down, Meghan."

Her daughter looked at Libby as if she'd lost her mind and in a way she supposed she had. That was the only thing that would explain how a toy—one she'd sworn she'd never seen before—could make her feel as if suddenly the walls were closing in on her. Her stomach churned.

"Don't worry. It doesn't look like he has fleas or anything." Meghan held the bear in front of her nose and studied him closely. "With a little cleaning and—"

"I told you, Meghan, put the bear down."

Libby's voice was sharp and prickly, and hearing it, she felt guilty for snapping and even guiltier for not caring.

"Come on. We're leaving." Libby swept past her daughter and toward the front door.

"But, Mom!" Meghan dropped the bear and shuffled behind. "We just got here. And it's not like I want to stay or anything but, gee, it's only a bear and it's nothing to get all nuts about."

No sooner was Meghan out on the porch than Libby closed the front door and locked it. It wasn't until she pocketed the key and turned to walk down the stairs that she realized there were tears in Meghan's eyes.

Libby's heart broke. She reached for her daughter's hand. "I'm sorry, honey. I didn't mean to snap at you. Maybe you were right and I was wrong. Maybe it was a mistake to come here after all." She took a deep breath. "I thought…"

"I know." Meghan gave her hand a squeeze. "I mean, I think I get it. Sort of. You thought you wouldn't care."

As insights went Libby wondered why she'd never thought of something so obvious herself. "I just didn't expect—"

"The bear, yeah. So what's the story?"

Libby had never lied to Meghan about her past. Oh, she didn't know the whole truth—that would be too much of a burden for any child her age. But when Meghan asked questions about Libby's childhood and about why Libby had been raised by the Palmers, her father's parents, Libby had never hesitated to give Meghan as much of the story as would satisfy her. As much as she could handle.

Libby wasn't about to start playing with the truth now.

"I'm not sure about the bear," Libby told her. "Not exactly, anyway. But there's something about him that makes me feel as if I've seen him before." A touch that felt like cold fingers skittered over her shoulders and Libby shivered. "I don't know," she said. "I know it sounds weird, but I think he used to be mine."

CHAPTER 3

They spent the night at an Embassy Suites, far from the dust they'd kicked up at the shop and the forgotten teddy bear that had created an avalanche of emotions that had both surprised and confounded Libby. She wasn't naive; she knew from the start that going to Cleveland might stir memories of her relationship with her mother. It was, after all, one of the reasons Libby had chosen to come in the first place. But after spending years repressing Barb's memory and all her energy fighting her emotional response to it, she simply hadn't expected to be knocked for a loop.

But then, she hadn't expected to run into the tattered teddy bear either.

Libby dealt with it. If there was one thing she'd learned in the months since Rick confessed to his relationship with Belinda, it was that she couldn't let her personal pain get in the way of what she needed to accomplish. If she was going to make a new start—and a new life—for Meghan and herself, she had to swallow her misgivings and get on with her plans. Number one on the list was to make Barb's Knits a viable business and the apartment upstairs a home.

With that in mind, she and Meghan stopped at a grocery store on the way in from the hotel the next morning and loaded up on paper towels and cleaning supplies. They bought a cooler, too, a bag of ice and a twelve-pack of soda. Not so good for Meghan's teeth but plenty good for parental PR, and after all Meghan had been through lately, it was the least Libby could do.

Back at the shop, she unlocked the front door and pushed it open.

"It smells better than it did yesterday."

It didn't; Meghan was only trying to make her feel better. After Libby propped the porch chair against the door to air out the store, she hugged her daughter just to let her know how much she appreciated the moral support.

Though it was early, the sky was gray and the clouds were heavy. As soon as she stepped inside, Libby hoisted the plastic bags of cleaning supplies onto the front counter and reached for the switch to flick on the lights.

Not a single one of them worked.

"And am I surprised?" she mumbled.

Meghan was apparently feeling braver than she had the day before. She headed off to explore. "Are you?" she called over her shoulder from a room off the middle showroom where a round wooden table was surrounded by chairs—and everything was coated in dust. "Surprised, that is?"

"Not even a little." Firmly ignoring the bear who was lying where he'd been dropped, Libby looked at the dust that covered the counters, the dirt that sat on the window-sills and the faded yarn that was everywhere. It was piled on tables and heaped in baskets. It was mounded on an old mahogany buffet and jammed onto the shelves of a bookcase that took up most of one wall in the former dining room. There was even yarn displayed in what used to be the kitchen. Every cupboard door had been removed and each shelf was filled with wool. Some of it still looked usable. Most of it looked old and sad. None of it looked clean. "Grandma Palmer always said Barb wasn't much of a house-keeper."

"Doesn't that seem bizarre?" Meghan had been looking through an old steamer trunk open on the floor and filled with yarn. The top layer of yarn had once been pastel colors and was now a uniform and dull shade of gray, but without sunlight to fade it and no coating of dust, the yarn beneath it had fared better. When Meghan stood, there was pink fuzz on her nose. She brushed it away with one finger. "That would be like me calling you Libby. No way you'd ever let me get away with it. Don't you feel weird calling your mom Barb?"

It was better to concentrate on the facts than it was to edi-torialize, so that's exactly what Libby did. "She wasn't much of a mom," she said. "You know all that, honey."

"Because she left you, and you were raised by your dad's

parents, Grandma and Grandpa P. I get it." Meghan nodded solemnly. As if she understood. As if, as a child who had spent her life with two parents who—in spite of their own personal differences—adored her, she possibly could. "Your mom... Barb...you told me had problems. Drug problems."

"It was the sixties and I guess things were different then. At least that's what people say. Anyway, I think Barb had her reasons. Remember, my dad was killed in a war."

Meghan nodded. "Vietnam. We talked about it in history class."

"Barb couldn't handle his death. She was depressed. Lonely. Probably scared, too." And before Rick walked out on her, Libby had never quite understood any of that. She'd spent years desperate to come to some understanding about her mother. She'd never thought it might come thanks to her own divorce.

It used to be that Barb and everything associated with her—their life together before she abandoned Libby, and the intriguing possibility of how things might have worked out differently—were the hardest things to think about. Back then, Libby thanked her lucky stars for Rick and the life they'd established together.

Funny, these days she thought about Barb when she wanted to forget about Rick.

"Things worked out best for me," she told Meghan, talking about her childhood, not about her divorce. As far as Libby was concerned, that story didn't have an ending. At least not yet. "Instead of being raised by a woman who probably didn't have the skills or the patience to be much of a mother, I got to live with Grandma and Grandpa P. And Grandma and Grandpa P...well, I think the only person they love more than me in the whole wide world is you."

Meghan took that much for granted, but that didn't keep her from smiling. Before the Palmers had retired to Arizona, she'd spent a great deal of time with them, and even though thousands of miles now separated them, there was no doubt she was still the light of their lives. "But doesn't that make you wonder...?" Meghan's dark brows dipped into a vee, the way they always did when she was considering something beyond her years or her understanding.

"What?"

Meghan shrugged. "It's nothing."

"It's something. Otherwise you wouldn't have brought it up."

"It's just that...I dunno..." She twirled one curl of her shoulder-length hair. "I just wondered, you know, why if Barb never even saw you, if she never talked to you since you were little, why she left you her business."

Libby might never have lied to her daughter, but that didn't mean she had always told the whole truth and nothing but. There were some details Meghan wasn't old enough to hear yet. Some details Libby didn't like to bring out into the light of day and examine, and rather than do it now, she stuck to the matter at hand. "I don't know why she left me her business," Libby admitted. "Maybe she felt guilty."

"About leaving you with Grandma P, you mean."

Libby nodded. "About that. About never calling or writing or—" She coughed away a sudden tightness in her throat. "I've told you all that, too," she said, feeling safer skirting the subject than she did being smack-dab in the quagmire. "I don't have any answers. Nobody does. I'm grateful she did leave the business to me, though. It's given us a place to start over. And I'm sorry that Barb's life was so out of control."

"Except if it was…" She shivered and hugged her arms around herself. "How did she ever keep the business going?" she asked. In spite of Libby's warning that, no matter what the calendar said, it was too damp and cool for summer clothes, Meghan had chosen to wear a pair of khaki shorts and a bright yellow tank.

Another look around the shop at the cobwebs and the dirt, and Libby found herself wondering the same thing. "I'm hoping we find some ledger books or something so we can find out how the business was really doing. Something tells me it wasn't doing well. Barb sure didn't keep this place in shape." As if to prove the theory, Libby saw a movement out of the corner of her eye. A mouse. Rather than freak Meghan out, she ignored the critter and promised herself a trip to a hardware store and a lifetime supply of traps. "This place is a mess."

"Kind of makes you wonder, doesn't it?" Meghan looked up toward the water-stained ceiling, and Libby knew exactly what she was thinking.

The day before, they had ventured no farther than the dining room, where the tattered teddy bear had been waiting for them. Today it was time to check out the apartment upstairs. She wondered what she'd find in the place Barb had called home. As to how she'd handle the glimpse into her mother's private world, Libby knew there was only one way to find out.

"Feeling brave?" she asked, and before Meghan could answer—and before Libby herself could listen to the voice inside her own head that asked if after all this time *she* was ready—she headed through the kitchen and to the stairway near the back door.

She took the steps two at a time, partly to make Meghan think this was all part of the adventure she'd promised but mostly because she knew if she dawdled, she'd lose her nerve.

She paused at the top of the steps, bracing herself. After Meghan arrived, though, there was only so long she could stall. A quick breath for courage, and Libby pushed open the door.

They found themselves in the kitchen, a small, tidy room painted sunny yellow with red accents. There was a maple table surrounded by four chairs against the windows to Libby's left, and a ceiling fan overhead. There was more dust, sure, but it wasn't what she *saw* that caught Libby's attention. It was what was *missing* from the room that piqued her curiosity.

Anxious to see if her initial suspicion was true, she did a

quick survey and made a trip through the kitchen and into the small spare dining room. From there, she peeked into the living room, the bedroom and the bath.

The apartment was orderly. The furniture wasn't flashy, but it was sturdy and well cared for. The colors were pleasant, brighter and clearer than what she'd expected, though she had to admit she honestly didn't know what she'd expected.

"It looks like no one ever lived here," Libby mumbled, testing the theory on herself. Just to be sure she wasn't imagining it, she looked around again. There were no pictures on the walls or on the end tables flanking the living room couch. There were no books on the shelves in the one corner of the bedroom that had apparently been used as an office. There was nothing in the way of mementos or knickknacks. No plants or candles or magazines left lying around.

Barb had died suddenly and certainly unexpectedly in an auto accident, and when she'd imagined this moment—as she had so many times—Libby had envisioned stepping into the apartment and directly into what had been her mother's life. There would be books, and the books would give Libby a clue as to whether Barb enjoyed romances or mysteries, thrillers or history. There would be magazines, and she'd find out if her mother was the *Newsweek* type or a woman who read *People*. There would be little clues in the kinds of photos Libby had expected to find dotting the apartment: vacations, friends, pets. Maybe a picture of Libby as a child?

The very thought clutched at her heart, and she turned

her back on Meghan and cleared her throat. "Somebody's been here," she said, though she suspected Meghan hadn't thought of that. Nor did she think her daughter cared. "No way could anyone live without anything personal at all. Somebody must have come in after Barb died and cleaned the place up. I wonder what they took?"

"You're not going to start that again, are you?" Meghan tried to keep her question light, but Libby couldn't help but notice the undertone of worry.

She turned and pinned her daughter with a look. "Start what?"

"You know…" Meghan shrugged, body language designed to let her mother know how little she cared. It didn't work. As soon as Meghan failed to meet her eyes, Libby knew something was bothering her. If she needed more proof, it came in the singsong bitterness of Meghan's voice. "You get the Subaru, I get the Lexus. I get the piano, you take the silver. You and Daddy…" Meghan kicked the toe of her sandals against the blue-and-white-tile floor. "Dividing up everything like it was the money and those little houses in a Monopoly game. Is that how you got stuck with me?"

As if she'd been punched, Libby sucked in a breath. "Where did that come from?"

Meghan turned away.

"Look…" She reached for her daughter's hand, and though Meghan tried to be aloof and adult she was, after all, just a little girl. When Libby tugged her, she melted into her mother's arms. One arm around her shoulders, Libby rubbed Meghan's back the way she used to all those years before when she'd perched on the edge of Meghan's bed and read her a bedtime story. "Divorce isn't easy for anyone," she said. "It wasn't easy for me, and…" She swallowed her pride; easing Meghan's fears was more important. "It wasn't easy for Daddy either. There are lots of decisions that have to be made when a marriage is over and, yes, some of those decisions involve material things. The cars and the piano and the silver…those were all things that belonged to both me and Daddy. That's why we had to decide who got what. Legally there was no other way. But you…" She held Meghan at arm's length and with one finger chucked her under the chin.

"There was no deciding about who wanted you and who didn't. We both did. We both do. That's why you're here in Cleveland with me now. And it's why you're going to spend as much time as possible with Daddy. We'd both like to have you with us all the time. But unless we can figure out how to clone you, that's just not going to work. We adore you, silly creature." When she coaxed a smile out of Meghan, Libby breathed easier. "No matter what else ever happens between me and Daddy, nothing will ever change that. You know that, don't you?"

Meghan wasn't about to give in easily. Not when she was the center of attention and being told how wonderful she was. "Did Barb ever tell you stuff like that?"

"No." Libby shook her head. "She never did. At least not that I remember. Maybe she just didn't want to make promises she couldn't keep."

"Promises like how you'll always love me and you'd never leave me the way she left you?"

Had the worry haunted Meghan all these years?

The very thought pierced Libby's heart and she prayed it wasn't true. She had never questioned the wisdom of sharing her story with Meghan, but she'd never meant to make her question if she was valued and loved.

No, Rick had done that when he walked out on both of them.

Rather than let her anger at Rick spoil the moment, Libby kissed Meghan's cheek. "I will never leave you like my mother left me," she told Meghan. "I would never even think of it. I'd never even think about thinking about it. I'd never even think about thinking about—"

"All right!" Meghan laughed, and Libby was glad. A child of divorce had enough to worry about without adding to the list.

"And when I talked about someone being here and taking things…just so you know, I'm not being greedy. I just wondered." Libby took another look around at the bare apartment and wondered what it had been like when Barb was alive. Did she host dinner parties in the dining room? And if she did, who did she invite? Did she have friends? Or a cheerless, lonely existence? If she'd been alone, was it Libby's fault?

That was too much to consider and Libby shook the thought away. "I just wondered what kind of things might have been here," she told Meghan.

"You mean stuff that would tell you what Barb was like."

Libby sighed in relief. Sometimes her daughter could be remarkably mature. "Exactly."

"Maybe we'll find something."

Another look around and Libby shook her head. "I'm not holding out a lot of hope for that."

"You never know." Meghan untangled herself from Libby and strolled into the living room. "You know," she raised her voice so Libby could hear her in the kitchen. It didn't take much; the apartment wasn't much bigger than the great room back in their suburban Cranberry Township home. "It's not as bad as I thought it would be up here. I mean, it's not nearly as nice as home, but…" Meghan moved aside the lace curtains on the living room window that looked over the street. "At least it's not as grungy as downstairs."

"It will be even nicer once we get it cleaned up and get some of our own stuff in here."

"Yeah. Except we have to share a bedroom." She thought her mother couldn't see her, but Libby didn't miss the face Meghan made. "How lame is that, having to share a room with your mother?"

"Once we get the business up and going, we might use the apartment for storage and move into a bigger place. Or we can think about adding onto the shop and giving you your own suite downstairs. How would that be?"

Meghan's blue eyes lit up. "Promise?"

"No." Meghan's hopeful expression fell and Libby laughed. "I can't promise, but I can plan. Right now our plan starts with getting things ready up here so we don't have to spend my entire divorce settlement on hotel bills." She looked around again at the apartment, filled with furniture but empty when it came to clues about her mother's life.

"At least it won't be as hard to clean up here as it will be down in the shop. I thought there would be more to pack up, things to cart away. I thought—"

Rick's words pounded through her head.

What are you hoping for? A letter? 'Dear Libby, here are all the reasons I abandoned you, now you can live happily ever after'?

"Damned straight," Libby mumbled to herself, then smiled at the look of utter bewilderment on Meghan's face when she realized her mother was talking to herself. "Don't worry, kid, I haven't lost my mind. I was just wishing that Barb had left us something."

"Some hint about who she really was and why she left you?"

"Now that you mention it…" Libby wrapped her arm around Meghan, and together they headed downstairs for the cleaning supplies. "I'd settle for an explanation as to why she left a yarn shop to a woman who can't knit!"

* * *

The next day, the first thing Libby discovered was that the air-conditioning didn't work. Too bad. The skies had finally cleared, the temperature was flirting with the mideighties and outside the sidewalks steamed with humidity.

She was hot. She was sweaty. She desperately needed a break from the mountain of cleaning that had kept her busy all morning.

So why, she asked herself, hadn't she chosen something a little more relaxing?

She flicked a bead of sweat off her forehead and scraped her palms against the legs of her black shorts. By the time she took a deep breath and reached for the blue metal knitting needles she'd found below the front counter that morning, her hands were as damp as ever.

Needles in her right hand, yarn in her left, she stared at the how-to pictures in the book she and Meghan had unearthed in the room beside the dining room, which must have once been Barb's classroom.

In fact, because that particular room wasn't nearly as cluttered as the rest of the store, and so, easier to organize, Libby had left Meghan in there to finish the cleaning.

"Sure you don't want to come over here and try this with me?" she called to her now. Meghan needed a break. And Libby? Well, she knew from the start that a little moral support in the knitting department wouldn't hurt. "It's a whole lot of fun."

"No, thanks." Meghan's voice floated back to Libby along with a plume of dust from the general direction of the classroom. "And don't tell me it's fun, Mom. No way do you sound like you're having fun."

"You got me there," Libby grumbled, but she wasn't about to give up. As if it actually might help her make sense of the instructions, she bent closer to the page. "Cast on?" She read the words in large, bold print and peered at the drawings and the instructions. None of it made sense. If she tried to ignore the written instructions and follow the drawings, she got confused. If she did exactly what the instructions said and didn't pay any attention to the drawings, she was more mixed up than ever.

After thirty minutes of trying, the only thing she'd succeeded in doing was putting a slipknot on one of the needles.

Something told her there was more to it than that.

Refusing to be intimidated by either the incomprehensible instructions, the confusing drawings or the needles that felt so foreign in her hands, Libby followed the pictures in the book, wound the yarn around her fingers and—

"Damn!" She watched the yarn untangle. Right before it settled into looking exactly the way it looked before she began the process.

She wondered if she was the only person in the world who'd ever had trouble learning to knit and decided that she must be. From the book's worn pages and tattered binding, she guessed it was something Barb or her customers had used a lot. Obviously the incomprehensible instructions and mystifying black-and-white drawings meant something to them, and just as obviously that meant they must have been far more intelligent and far less klutzy than Libby.

With a sigh, she flipped the book closed. It was, according to its title, a complete and comprehensive guide to knitting, and as far as she could tell, the complete and comprehensive part was true. At the back of the heavy volume there were pictures of different stitch patterns and instructions on how to knit them, written in what looked to be some kind of code. There was a section on the different kinds of knitting needles—a surprise to Libby since she didn't know there *were* different kinds of knitting needles—and another on choosing the right yarn for every project. There were chapters on finishing garments and fixing mistakes.

Comprehensive was the name of the game.

As for being a guide, Libby was pretty certain two-dimensional drawings designed to teach her a three-dimensional skill weren't going to guide her anywhere but to frustration.

So far it was the only thing about knitting she was good at.

"Mom! You said this was going to be easy." Meghan's anguished cry pretty much echoed the words that were bouncing through Libby's head. Meghan, though, was not talking about knitting. Libby looked up just in time to see her daughter come through the dining room dragging two very full black garbage bags. "It doesn't look like there's much junk in there. Until you start digging through it all. There was tons of paper in that cabinet against the wall. And there was plenty of yarn piled in those baskets in there. What do you want me to do with this junk?"

At breakfast they'd discussed their cleaning and organizing strategy over muffins from the nearby bakery shop, but she wasn't surprised that Meghan didn't remember. Even as Libby had listed their tasks room by room, and looked at a calendar to set a schedule so they could have the store cleaned out before the end of summer, she knew Meghan wasn't listening and knew precisely why. Cleaning out years of clutter from a dusty and dreary yarn shop was not Meghan's idea of fun.

Libby appreciated the help more than she could say. That was the only thing that made it possible for her to force the knitting-induced aggravation out of her voice. "Is that good junk or bad junk in those bags?" she asked.

Her daughter rolled her eyes. Libby was quickly learning this was an all-embracing expression, a sort of universal language practiced by every teenager on the face of the earth. It could mean anything from *You've got to be kidding* to *How could I possibly be this smart when I have a mother who is so dumb?* and everything in between.

This time she was pretty certain the expression covered the smart/dumb part of the equation.

Libby massaged her temples with the tips of her fingers. "You remember what we said this morning? If it's just dusty, there might be something we can do to salvage the yarn. Or maybe we can at least donate it somewhere and take the tax write-off. But if it's got mouse dirt on it, well, in that case we're going to have to toss it."

"This is some kind of sick joke, right? You expect me to check to see if there's mouse poop on this yarn?" Meghan's face turned as pale as her white T-shirt. She'd been clutching one garbage bag in each dirty fist and now she dropped them and stepped back. "That's too disgusting for words! There is no way I'm going to do that. There's no way I should have to! If I was home—"

"You are home."

"Oh, yeah, right. I forgot. We left our nice house and our nice neighborhood so we could live in the ghetto. We spend our time looking for mouse poop."

"Meghan…" Libby made a move to walk around the front counter, but Meghan would have none of it. She backed up another step. If that's the way Meghan wanted it, Libby wouldn't violate her space. "Why don't you take a break? You could go upstairs and—"

"And that's supposed to make me feel better?"

It was a rhetorical question and Libby knew better than to answer it. Rhetorical questions from testy teenagers meant nothing but trouble.

"Go!" she said instead, and somehow when she shooed Meghan toward the back of the store, she managed to make it look like a casual gesture instead of the ultimate surrender. "I don't care what you do up there, just do something that will help make it easier when the movers arrive with our fur-

niture next week. I'll look through the yarn myself and decide
what to do with it."

"Yeah, go right ahead. Have fun looking for mouse poop."

Meghan's final comments rang through the store along
with the sounds of her footsteps as she stomped up the steps.
The last Libby heard from her was the slam of the upstairs door.

"You handled that well," Libby told herself, the sarcasm as
heavy as the bags she grabbed and dragged to the corner of
the room. "A few more years of practice and you really ought
to know how to screw up a conversation with your daughter."

The possibilities were too frightening to dwell on, and
besides, she didn't have the time or the energy. Libby went
back to the front counter, but there was nothing appealing
about trying to knit again. Instead she reached for the legal
pad where earlier that day she'd begun a to-do list.

So far not one thing was checked off.

Upstairs
Finish cleaning.

Downstairs
Sort through all yarn and knitting supplies, toss what
can't be saved.
Catalogue and store the rest in moth-proof containers.
Thoroughly clean.
Repair ceiling in dining room.
Paint.

Talk to yarn companies, schedule visits from reps.

Stock shelves.

Talk to bank.

Meet with attorney.

Arrange for advertising.

Plan grand opening.

Set date for soft opening.

Just looking at the list, a thread of panic snaked through her. She beat it back with reason. It would take a lot longer than one morning to make a difference in the disaster that was Barb's Knits. She and Meghan had made a start, she reminded herself, and if Meghan didn't want to participate...

She looked up at the ceiling, wondering what her daughter was doing upstairs. Was she busy putting their room in some sort of order or was she up there sulking?

Either way, Libby wasn't worried. Meghan would eventually realize she'd be more comfortable if the room she and Libby shared looked at least a little like her room had back at home. She'd want her clothes in neat order in her half of the closet and the little bit of makeup Libby allowed her—lip gloss and light pink nail polish—displayed on her dresser.

Sooner or later Meghan would come around. At least Libby hoped she would.

As for Barb's Knits, that was another matter altogether.

"It won't come around at all. Not unless I make it come around," Libby told herself. With that in mind, she'd just started to flip through the calendar to check their cleaning schedule when she heard a bang, a crash and the sound of breaking glass upstairs. All of it was punctuated by Meghan's high-pitched scream.

Libby's heart jumped into her throat. She had raced through the store and up the stairs before she realized she was even moving. "Meghan? Meghan, answer me. Are you all right? What happened? What—"

She pushed open the kitchen door and found Meghan standing in the middle of the room, covered with plaster dust. She was holding the metal pull chain that belonged to the ceiling fan. The fan itself—or at least what was left of it—was on top of the kitchen table along with about a million shards of glass that sparkled like diamonds in the morning sunlight. The acrid smell of fried electrical wires filled the air.

"I'm sorry!" Meghan must have mistaken Libby's expression for anger instead of the relief it was. Meghan's face was coated with plaster dust, and when she started to cry, the tears left rivulets on her cheeks. "I didn't mean it, Mom. I was just trying to turn the fan on. It's hot and there's no air-conditioning and—" The rest of her words were lost in a wail of despair.

"It's okay, honey. Honest." Libby did a quick assessment of her daughter's condition. Except for a cut on her arm, it didn't look as if Meghan had sustained any injuries. The fan and the ceiling it had once been anchored to were another matter. One Libby would deal with after she took care of Meghan.

She led her to the bathroom. "It's no big deal. We'll get the fan fixed."

Meghan was beyond being consoled. She was scared, she was shocked and she was embarrassed as only a fourteen-year-old can be. She was crying so hard Libby could barely understand her. "And the ceiling? How are you going to fix the ceiling? It fell down right on top of me. I hate it here. Mommy, please, please let's go home!"

It was the worst time in the world for the phone to ring. Libby left Meghan in the bathroom to wash her face and hands and grabbed the phone.

"Mrs. Cartwright! How's everything going there?" It took her a moment to recognize the voice of Will Harper, the real-estate agent. "You enjoying our fair city?"

Libby looked at the wreckage in the kitchen. "It's not exactly a good time to be asking that," she said. "We're having a little electrical problem here."

"I'm not surprised." She could picture Will shaking his head in an I-told-you-so way. "That property has seen better days."

Meghan was still crying and Libby could barely hear. She retreated into the living room. "What can I do for you, Mr. Harper?"

Will laughed. "Oh, no. That's not what you're supposed to be asking. I've called, Mrs. Cartwright, because I'm going to do something for you."

"Like?"

"Like admitting you were right and I was wrong. Doesn't happen often, let me tell you. I know this market like the back of my hand."

"And—"

Meghan peeked into the room. She saw that Libby was on the phone so she didn't talk loud—at least not too loud—when she wailed, "I can't find the bandages anywhere!"

Libby trailed into the bathroom, sure they'd unpacked a first-aid kit the day before. She looked in the medicine cabinet and on the shelves under the sink. She checked the linen closet in the hallway.

"I'm sorry," she said when she remembered that she still had the phone to her ear. "You've caught us at a bad time. You were saying…." She found the first-aid kit under a stack of towels, flipped it open and whisked out a bandage. She handed it to Meghan at the same time she whispered, "Put some antibacterial ointment on that first," and then got back to her conversation. "About the market?"

"I was saying that you were right and I was wrong. You see, Mrs. Cartwright, I just heard from the Tip-Top folks. You had them pegged from the get-go. You turned down their initial offer and as it turned out, so did the folks who own the other property they were considering. You're a genius. You caught them between a rock and a hard place. They just called me. They've upped their offer."

"More money? How much?"

Meghan couldn't have had any idea who she was talking to, but she did have a sixth sense as to what they were talking about. She sniffed and hurried over to where Libby was standing. She jumped up and down, her hands folded in supplication.

"Please!" Meghan knew better than to take the chance of disrupting the deal and kept her voice at a stage whisper. "It's those drugstore people, isn't it? Please take the offer, Mom. Let's get out of here."

Libby hushed her. It was hard to listen to both Will Harper and Meghan, but she did catch the figure. It was fifteen thousand dollars more than Tip-Top had originally offered, nearly all her original asking price.

"It's a gift," Will said.

"Maybe, but—"

"But you've seen the property, Mrs. Cartwright. You're there now, right?"

"I am, but—"

"You really think you'll be able to clean up that mess?"

She did. At least she had until the ceiling fell down.

Libby's shoulders drooped with the weight of the reality that seemed to crash down along with the ceiling fan. Sure, she'd had great plans for the place and, yes, she'd had every intention of carrying through with them. But now…

She looked into the kitchen at the pieces of glass that littered the place like confetti. She remembered the endless to-do list down on the front counter. And the mice. She thought of how, in spite of what she'd hoped, there wasn't one clue about Barb or her life anywhere. A trickle of sweat glided between her shoulder blades. She read the desperation in her daughter's eyes.

"Give me twenty-four hours," she told Will. "Let me sleep on it. Tomorrow I'll let you know for sure if I'm going to stay. Or take the offer from Tip-Top."

CHAPTER 4

One more night in a hotel wouldn't blow their budget.

At least not completely.

Libby set the ice bucket on the machine at the end of the hallway that led to their room at the Embassy Suites and lectured herself: she had nothing to feel guilty about; it was just one more night; and after their disastrous day, she and Meghan deserved a little TLC, not to mention some air-conditioning.

She pressed the button on the front of the machine and watched as the ice crashed into the bucket below. Her shoulders ached. Her head pounded. There was ceiling plaster in her hair and her scalp itched. Her fingers were sore from the tiny cuts that had resulted from picking up the last bits of glass in the kitchen that refused to be corralled by the broom and dustpan. She was dog-tired, and if the expressions on the faces of the folks behind the front desk when she and Meghan walked in meant anything, Libby had a sneaky suspicion the two of them looked like earthquake refugees.

"One more night," she told herself. "And tomorrow—"

She thought back to her conversation with Will and congratulated herself. She had been firm with him. At least as firm as any woman could be who had just seen her kitchen ceiling crumble, her budget—now that she had a ceiling to fix—blasted to hell, her daughter freak and her plans for a neat and orderly move go up in smoke and with the smell of burning electrical wires. Still, she hadn't given in to the temptation of a knee-jerk response and instantly accepted the new offer. That was a good thing. Wasn't it?

Of course, she had promised she'd talk to Will the next day, and one of the hard lessons she'd learned in the days since Rick told her he'd never really understood what love was all about until he met Belinda was that tomorrow always came. Whether she wanted it to or not.

"Maybe Will is right," Libby said, not caring that she was talking to herself. There was no one around, and even if there was, one look at her and they'd probably assume she was crazy anyway. "Maybe we should just cut and run. It's the smart thing to do. It's the logical thing to do. And if it isn't what Barb wanted…"

She propped the ice bucket in the crook of her arm and trudged down the hallway, pausing outside the door to their room. From inside she could hear Meghan's voice. She *was* on the phone.

What Barb wanted…

What Barb didn't want…

That shouldn't have entered into her mind in the first place; she had no way of knowing what Barb really wanted and it looked as if she'd never know. If Barb had wanted to give Libby some sort of insight into her life and help Libby get to know her better, that wasn't ever going to happen. Thirty-some years of absence and a cleaned-out apartment had made sure of that.

And what did it matter anyway? What difference would it make now?

As they had so many times before for so many years, the questions pounded through Libby's head.

Until now, she'd always held out hope—preposterous or not—that she would come to some understanding of her mother's life. That she would someday be at peace with Barb's decisions. A trip to Barb's Knits was Libby's own personal quest for the Holy Grail, her chance to get as up close and personal as she could with the woman she'd last seen—

"Don't go there," she warned herself, and as she had done so expertly before, she put the thought out of her head. Call it a twist of fate. Or just a sick trick played by a brain that was mush and a body that was exhausted beyond being able to care. No sooner had one memory been suppressed than another surfaced. It was vague and disjointed, as memories often are, seen through the eyes of a child but processed now by an adult who wondered how much of it was real and how much had been distorted and repositioned into new shapes like the bits of glass in a kaleidoscope.

* * *

"Don't go far, honey!"

In her mind, Libby could see Barb standing at the end of a grocery store aisle. Her dark hair spilled over her shoulders. Her skirt, with its swirls of green and red and blue, was so long it was hard to see that her feet were bare. There was a white carnation tucked behind her ear, and she was wearing the red-and-blue beads Libby had strung for her at a street fair. Barb's eyes were bloodshot, and she swayed the way she did when she played the Beatles or the Rolling Stones on the record player in the living room and she held Libby's hands as they danced around in a circle.

"You stay close." Barb's words were dreamy, and she wasn't watching her daughter when she spoke. Her eyes were on the tall man who stood at her side. He was as skinny as the green beans Grandma Palmer served at Sunday dinner, and his hair was the color of straw. It was longer than Barb's.

Try as she might, Libby couldn't recall his name. She wondered if she ever knew it. She was certain, though, that Barb had spent a lot of time with the man. She had a blurred recollection of long afternoons when Barb and the man stayed in his bedroom while Libby watched *Sesame Street*. And flashes of memory that featured the man on the guitar and Barb singing "Puff the Magic Dragon." Libby knew that they spent a lot of their time smoking pot because the first time she smelled it in her college dorm she immediately flashed back to that day in the grocery store and the sweet scent that had clung to her mother's clothes.

In her mind's eye, she watched Barb wind her fingers through the man's. She saw the way he leaned forward and whispered in Barb's ear. She heard her mother laugh.

"You're a wild man!" Barb didn't say it as if it was a bad thing. She grabbed one end of the long scarf she'd knitted out of black wool and kissed the man on the mouth, right under his bushy mustache. "One of these days, you're going to get me in real trouble."

Barb and the man hurried down the snack aisle, and the memory ended abruptly. It picked up again with a sense of anxiety and a mother's knowledge that the little girl who had grown into Libby was tired and bored. It must have been past dinnertime; of all the insignificant things to remember about a day that had changed her life, Libby remembered being hungry.

She also remembered the way her throat tightened and her stomach bunched when she lost sight of her mother. The beginnings of a full-scale tantrum built.

Libby was not an emotional child. It never occurred to her to be dramatic. Rather than yell, she walked around the store, and by the time she got back to where she'd started, her feet hurt and her legs were tired. She was hungrier than ever.

As clearly as if it were yesterday, she remembered eying the shelf where the chocolate-chip cookies were displayed.

It was high and she couldn't reach it. She must have been carrying something—though she couldn't have said what—because she remembered setting that something down. With two hands free, she swept aside the packages of pretzels on the shelf closest to the floor and climbed. She could see over the edge of the cookie shelf, but her arms weren't long enough to reach. She stretched, and her elbow knocked against boxes of graham crackers. They hit the floor.

Libby stretched some more. Finally her fingers met their mark. She clung to a package of cookies and pulled. By the time she was settled on the green tile floor again and had a cookie in her mouth and another one in her hand, she heard a voice from the end of the aisle.

"There!"

Libby looked up to see a lady pushing a shopping cart and standing next to a man in a blue shirt. He was frowning.

The lady pointed at Libby. "I told you, Greg, she's running around the store like a wild Indian. No one's watching her. She's bound to get into trouble."

"Or to get hurt." Greg hurried over to where Libby stood in the wreckage of graham cracker boxes and cookie crumbs. He bent down and looked her in the eye. "Hey, little girl, what's your name? And where's your mommy?"

Libby didn't answer. To this very day, she felt the certainty of her decision. She didn't have to say a word. After all Barb was in the store and pretty soon she'd show up and explain that Libby was her little girl.

Her eyes round and that extra cookie tucked behind her back, Libby waited.

Barb didn't come.

Libby looked down the long aisle in both directions.

She didn't see Barb or hear the sound of her laugh.

Her mouth was dry. Her tummy rumbled. "Mommy?" she said, but suddenly her throat was knotted, her voice came out too quiet for Barb to hear. "Mommy?" she called again, louder this time.

Greg stood and looked in every direction. "I don't see your mommy around," he said. "But don't worry, we'll make an announcement over the PA system. Do you know your mommy's name?"

"There was a woman." The lady with the shopping cart craned her neck to look toward the front of the store. "I saw her a while ago. She was with that young man. You must have seen him. The one with all the hair." She clicked her tongue. "Hippies," she said, sounding like Grandma Palmer did when she said it.

"Those two?" Another woman came around the corner. She glanced over her shoulder at the big front windows that looked out at the parking lot. "They just left. No more than a minute ago. You don't suppose they could have—"

"Mommy?" Libby darted forward, but she didn't get far. The man with the blue shirt scooped her into his arms.

"We can't have you running all over Pittsburgh by yourself," he said. "What do you say, ladies?" He plunked

Libby down in the shopping cart among rolls of toilet paper, bags of apples and six cans of tomato soup. "You'll stay right here with her, won't you? I'm going to call the police."

Had Libby been paying attention, she would have known exactly what was happening. As it was, she watched in horror as the white van she recognized as Barb's boyfriend's cruised by the front windows and pulled out of the parking lot and onto the street.

Her eyes filled with tears and the tantrum she'd been holding back burst with the force only a four-year-old could muster.

"Mommy!" Libby's voice rose in panic, volume and velocity. "Mommy! Mommy!"

Libby sucked in a breath, steeling herself against the sharp pain of her memories. She wasn't sure if they were genuine or the product of an imagination that had had years to fill in the blanks. She wasn't sure it mattered.

Barb hadn't so much abandoned her in that grocery store as she'd simply forgotten her. Libby often wondered if Barb felt bad about what had happened. She didn't know for sure, she only knew that soon after, Barb signed over her parental privileges to Grandma and Grandpa P and effectively ended any relationship she'd ever had with her daughter.

So what was Libby trying to prove with this crazy quest of hers? What was she trying to salvage?

Barb's Knits?

Barb's life?

Barb's legacy?

Maybe it took the trip to Cleveland and a big dose of reality to bring Libby's brain finally into focus. Her search for information about her mother was nothing more than a daydream. And selfish. Wasn't Meghan's future more important than Libby's past? Wasn't Meghan's happiness more important than Libby's broken dreams?

Wasn't Meghan all that mattered?

Libby never put her decision into words, but even before she pushed open the hotel room door, she knew she'd made up her mind. She stepped inside, ready to announce the news to Meghan, but her daughter was still on the phone. It was clear she was talking to Rick, and for reasons she couldn't explain, Libby felt as if she was eavesdropping. She went into the bathroom and set the ice bucket down in the sink. Eavesdropping or not, it was impossible not to hear what Meghan was saying.

"It's awful, that's how it is." Libby didn't need to see Meghan to know she was rolling her eyes. "I'd way rather live with you and Belinda. At least you don't live in the ghetto."

There was quiet as Rick responded and Libby could only imagine what her ex was saying. Though he'd never bought into Libby's plan of moving to Cleveland and reopening the yarn shop, he'd never come right out and told his daughter that Libby was crazy either. At least as far as Libby knew. In his own way, Rick supported her. Even if he did it simply to make Meghan feel better.

"I know, I know," Meghan finally said. "But don't worry, Daddy. I won't have to put up with it much longer. That's what I called to tell you. That real-estate agent called Mom again today. He offered her more money."

Meghan paused and listened to what her father had to say.

"I don't think so," she responded. "I know we're going to come home really soon."

This was a surprising comment since Meghan didn't know what Libby had decided herself only moments earlier as she'd stood in the hallway engulfed in memory: she was going to take the offer.

Curious as to how Meghan already knew this, she stepped out of the bathroom. From there she could see Meghan sitting on the bed nearest the window. Her back was to the door; she didn't know Libby was there.

Meghan clicked her tongue. "Come on, Daddy, you know what I'm talking about. Mom's Mom, and you know how she is. She's going to give up. She always does, doesn't she? I've heard you say it yourself. When the going gets tough, Mom always quits."

Was it true?

The question hit like a punch to the stomach, and Libby staggered back against the wall.

Was she a quitter?

It was what Rick had told her the day he announced he was laying her off, the day he told her he didn't love her anymore. It was, apparently, how her daughter thought of her.

And the realization hurt more than she could say.

Libby struggled to catch her breath. She told herself the tears that sprang to her eyes were because she was tired. They were because she was frustrated by all she had to do, because she was in a strange city, far from home. But even as she repeated the words in her head, hoping to believe them, she knew she was lying to herself. Just as she knew that the truth was far less complicated than any of that.

Libby *was* a quitter—pure and simple. It wasn't until she heard it put so clinically and so coldly that reality hit home.

A sob escaped her and she muffled it, one hand over her mouth.

When the going gets tough, Mom always quits.

Meghan's words filled her head along with a vision of Rick on the other end of the phone, nodding in agreement. Of course her bailing at the first sign of inconvenience or trouble wouldn't have come as news to him. He was the person who knew her faults best. So well, in fact, that he'd chosen another woman to take her place in his home, in his bed and in his heart.

As it had so many times in the past months, the awareness hurt like a blow. Libby thought about all in the places in her life where she'd proved herself unworthy of Rick's love and undeserving of her daughter's admiration. None of them were major—the book discussion group, the yoga classes that had gotten in the way of Meghan's schedule, the garden that had turned from glorious to overgrown once she'd taken the job in Rick's office and didn't have the time to keep it in shape. Little by little, all the things that made Libby who she was were replaced by her daughter's wants and her husband's needs.

Even when Rick told her about Belinda and about the baby he was going to have with her, Libby hadn't put up much of a fight. Rick's needs had come first, and Libby had simply watched the train wreck unfold.

She'd quit.

The thought weighed heavily on her, and Libby's shoulders slumped. Through it all, she'd never once whined. After Belinda came along and ruined what she'd thought was a solid marriage and a perfect family, she didn't have the energy. But even before, she never would have dreamed of complaining. She'd loved her husband and she loved her daughter, and when their needs had crowded her schedule, there was always something—some little piece of Libby—that she was able to leave behind.

In return, she'd never asked for thanks. Nor had she ever expected any. But appreciation, that was something else. Now to find out that the only message she'd sent was that of giving up…

Was it any wonder Meghan expected her mother to live up to her reputation?

Libby wasn't sure how long she stood there, only that by

the time she realized she needed a tissue—badly—Meghan was off the phone and had turned on the TV. She ducked into the bathroom to blow her nose and examined her own reflection in the mirror.

The woman staring back at her with solemn brown eyes was nearly forty.

She was divorced.

She was alone.

Except for her daughter, she had nothing but the memory that she had once thought she'd grow old living side by side with Rick, the man she'd loved for what felt like forever.

Nothing except—

Libby drew in a breath and let it out slowly.

It wasn't like her to make up her mind in the blink of an eye. Not about anything. Yet if she ever had a chance to think back on this moment, she was sure that was how she'd remember it. She blew her nose one more time, splashed cold water on her face and headed out of the bathroom.

"You done with the phone?" she asked Meghan, and when her daughter nodded, she reached for her purse. "We'll head out for dinner in a couple minutes. I just want to make a quick call."

When Meghan saw her retrieve Will Harper's card, her eyes lit up and she squirmed with excitement the way Libby had seen her do on so many Christmas mornings. "You're calling now?" Meghan hopped off the bed and hurried over to where Libby stood next to the desk by the window. "You're the best, Mom. You're the smartest and the prettiest and the coolest mom ever!"

"I am, aren't I?" Libby punched in the number and got Will's voice mail. No surprise there; she knew he was a busy man. "Mr. Harper, it's me, Libby Cartwright. I know I said I'd call you tomorrow, but I figured there was no use waiting."

She made sure she kept her eyes on Meghan and a smile on her face as she delivered the rest of her message. "You can tell Tip-Top there's no way I'll accept the offer. Not any offer. We're here and we're staying."

Even when she saw Meghan's mouth drop open, she kept her smile firmly in place. "I appreciate all you've done for me, Mr. Harper, and I know you won't understand, but I'm not going to change my mind. After all…" Libby pulled in a deep breath and let it out slowly, making peace with the decision. "This time, I refuse to quit."

CHAPTER 5

Libby never second-guessed her decision.

At least not intentionally.

Then again, it was hard not to wonder—inadvertently, of course, and only in those moments when her guard was down or she was feeling overwhelmed by the shop and the apartment and everything that needed to be done to make both decent—if she hadn't completely lost her mind.

"Can't lose what you never had," she reminded herself, and smiling wryly, she sunk her arms elbow-deep back into a bucket of hot, sudsy water.

In the week that had passed since she told Will Harper she'd made up her mind once and for all—and reinforced that message the half dozen times he'd called just to make sure—she had completely emptied Barb's Knits. It was a monumental task, sure, and as dirty as any job she'd ever done, but she never stopped to consider how much work it was or how much her muscles ached. It was one major project out of the way and the satisfaction she got from checking it off her list made it all worthwhile.

As for Meghan…

On her hands and knees on the bare wood floor, Libby glanced toward the classroom where Meghan was supposed to be taking the packages of notions—scissors, tape measures, knitting needles—dusting each one and sorting them into their own separate boxes. Once the shop was thoroughly washed and the whole place was painted…

Libby pursed her lips to blow a curl of hair out of her eyes. It would have been easier if it wasn't hot, she wasn't sweaty and her hair didn't stick to her forehead as if it were glued to it.

Once all the cleaning and prep work was done and Libby ordered new yarn, pattern books and some of the fun and funky polka-dot knitting bags she'd seen in a manufacturer's catalogue, they would unpack what they'd salvaged and put everything on display.

None of it was easy, and Libby wasn't about to lie to herself and pretend it was. Easy didn't matter. Then again, stressful did, and the whole process would have been less nerve-racking if Meghan would just cooperate.

As if in response to Libby's thoughts, she heard a noise like an avalanche from the classroom.

"You all right, Meggie?" she called.

Except for a grumbled comment about slippery packing and stupid knitting needles that wouldn't stay put when she stacked them where she wanted them, her daughter didn't answer.

Then again, what did Libby expect? In the last week,

their furniture had arrived, they'd said goodbye to their room at the Embassy Suites and hello to their new home, in the apartment upstairs. The abstract concept of moving was officially a reality. Meghan was officially, thoroughly and completely pissed. As only a fourteen-year-old can be.

It was another thing Libby didn't allow herself to think about. Someday Meghan would understand the move was for the best. And until that someday came?

Libby could just about feel the wall of anger Meghan had built around herself. It was like a force field, and trying to involve Meghan in planning a grand-opening party, looking through yarn catalogues and deciding on paint colors hadn't breached it. Building a sense of ownership by having her help with the cleaning apparently wasn't working either. When Meghan wasn't sulking or complaining, she'd taken to disappearing up into the attic, where she spent long hours doing—according to what she said when Libby asked about it—"nothing."

And being hurt by Meghan's attitude, her disappearing act and the stinging remarks she tossed back in response to Libby's every question wasn't going to change a thing.

Reminding herself not to forget that, Libby finished the floor in the front room of the shop. Even without the fresh coat of polyurethane she'd apply once the humidity decreased from rain forest levels, it already looked better. Gratified that even a task this small was complete, she hoisted the heavy bucket and headed for the basement where she would empty it, refill and start on the floor in the next room. She had just stepped into what used to be the kitchen when she realized there was a woman standing near the back door.

Startled, Libby stopped short just inside the doorway. "Can I help you?"

The woman was even shorter than Libby and twice as heavy, and though Libby would have guessed her age at somewhere around seventy, it was hard to tell for certain. Her face was as round as an apple and, as often happens with older women who are overweight, her skin was smooth and unwrinkled. She was wearing an orange sundress that skimmed the tops of her pudgy knees, and her hair was cut short and colored a startling shade of red.

She smiled. "That's what I'm supposed to ask you, honey."

Libby didn't understand and the look on her face spoke volumes.

"Gwen," the woman said by way of introduction. "I live nearby. I brought you a little welcoming present." She pointed to a china platter she'd left on the nearest counter next to a stack of items—including the beat-up teddy bear— that Libby had yet to toss. Beneath plastic wrap Libby saw peanut butter cookies.

"Thank you." Her response was automatic. So was her embarrassment when she realized she was being less than gracious. She lowered the heavy bucket to the floor and wiped her hands against the legs of her jeans. "You'll have to forgive me, I'm in the middle of cleaning and I didn't expect visitors. Or customers." Panic welled in her. "You're not a customer, are you? Because I don't want to turn away a customer, but there's no way I'm ready yet. Not for customers. There's no yarn and no books and the knitting needles are all over the place and—"

"Not a problem." Gwen shrugged away her concern. "I didn't come to shop, so don't worry about that. And I don't mean to be a pest. Just wanted to stop by and check you out. I'm surprised I'm the first. The whole neighborhood is talking about you."

Mortified, Libby squeezed her eyes shut. "You mean because of all those garbage bags on the front lawn yesterday. I know. I'm so sorry. It was a mess, wasn't it? I had to do something with all the yarn we couldn't keep, and tossing it, well, that was the only thing I could think to do. But check it out...." She looked over her shoulder toward the front windows and the strip of lawn that just a few hours earlier had been awash in black garbage bags. "The city took it all. Every last bag. And I'm never going to be throwing away as much again, and—"

Gwen's laugh interrupted her. "Oh, honey, lighten up!" There was a shopping bag on the floor next to Gwen's feet, and she reached into it and pulled out an electric teakettle. "Figured you wouldn't be ready for company so I brought my own stuff," she said and she filled the kettle at the sink and plugged it in. "You look like you could use a break."

"I do. I could." There was something about Gwen that

made Libby feel a bit off center. She wasn't quite sure how she was supposed to treat her. For a potential customer or a casual visitor, she was awfully familiar with the place.

Gwen hurried to the other side of the room and the one cupboard Libby had yet to clean out. She'd done a quick inventory, though, and she knew it contained a couple tablecloths, a coffee carafe and serving pieces. Gwen, it seemed, knew exactly what she was after. She came back across the room holding a tea cozy knitted in thick blue yarn and accented with vivid purples in shades from grape to magenta. The cozy was shaped like a half circle with a hole on each side, one for the spout of a teapot and another for the handle. After the kettle whistled, she fished a pretty antique pot out of the bag she'd brought with her, poured water into it, dropped in three tea bags and set the cozy over the top of it. Finished, she unwrapped the cookies and offered the platter to Libby.

"The shop is looking good," Gwen said.

Libby wasn't so sure. She wrinkled her nose and took a cookie. "You think? There's a long way to go and a lot we need to get done." After she'd emptied the cupboards in the kitchen where yarn had been displayed, she'd realized a couple of the shelves were broken, and automatically her gaze traveled that way. "From the looks of things, it's a wonder how the place ever stayed in business."

Gwen didn't reply. In fact, she didn't do anything but stare at Libby as if something she'd said was particularly interesting. Or she was waiting for Libby to try a cookie.

Since Libby hadn't said anything that was even mildly thought-provoking, she took a bite of the cookie and nodded her approval. As peanut-butter cookies went, this one was truly amazing.

"The rest of the place is even worse," she said, somehow feeling as if she needed to defend her position. "There's water damage to the ceiling in the next room, and the shelves in the front room are loose. If I put any books on them, they'll crash to the floor. The whole place needs a coat of paint, the windows rattle and upstairs…" She sighed, thinking of the hole in the ceiling above the kitchen table. "Like I said, it's hard to imagine a place like this ever attracted any sort of paying clientele."

"You don't think it always looked this way, do you?" Gwen's question was as penetrating as her look, and when Libby didn't answer, she laughed. "Oh, honey, we do have a lot to talk about! Come on." She grabbed the teapot and put it on the vintage fifties Formica table in the center of the room along with two mugs, a small carton of milk and a few bags of sugar with the McDonald's logo on them. "Sit down. We'll have a cup of tea and talk." Gwen chuckled and her cheeks got pinker. "I'm really being pushy, aren't I? Maybe I should explain—I used to work here."

"With Barb?"

Gwen's eyes widened. Was she surprised by the question?

Not as surprised as Libby was that it popped out before she even had a chance to think about it. She sat in one of the kitchen chairs, but she didn't relax. Gwen's tantalizing comment sent a current of electricity through her and she held her breath, waiting for the older lady to reply.

Gwen took her time, pouring tea into each of the mugs. "That's not why they're talking, you know," she said, and it took Libby a moment to realize she had changed the subject. "The people around here, they're not talking about you because of all the garbage. No way. You, honey, are a neighborhood hero."

As compliments went, it was nice, but Libby didn't much care. Not when she was this close to talking to someone who'd actually known Barb and worked with her. Distracted, she nodded. "Because of Tip-Top."

Gwen settled herself in the chair across from hers. "Your property sits dead in the center of the block, and it's the whole block they wanted. Thanks for not giving in."

"I don't imagine the folks on either side of me are especially thrilled." Libby looked both ways. "I hear Peg at the beauty shop was all set to sell."

Gwen shrugged. "She'll get over it. Where would she go anyway? Her only son lives in one of those hoity-toity suburban condos. Peg would hate it there. She couldn't walk to the corner for her nightly shot and a beer." Gwen ripped open three bags of sugar, dumped them into her cup and grabbed one of the spoons she'd brought with her. "People around here, they're thrilled that you didn't cave in to those Tip-Top folks."

"Would Barb have done the same thing?"

The twinkle in Gwen's eyes told Libby she wasn't easily fooled. Gwen knew Libby wasn't interested in neighborhood politics. "She wouldn't have given those drugstore people the time of day. She loved this neighborhood and she loved this place."

Not for the first time since Gwen walked into the shop, Libby found herself questioning the older lady's comments and the evidence in front of her own eyes. She remembered the mouse she'd found in the trap under the sink that morning. And the front door she'd yet to clean because she feared that once the dirt was washed off there'd be nothing left to hold the door together.

She didn't so much distrust what Gwen was saying as she suspected there was some revisionist history at work.

"I'm not one to tell stories out of school," Gwen said and she laughed. "Well, actually, I am. And I'll tell you what—I don't know how well you knew that real-estate agent who listed this property, but he's the one responsible for the way it looks."

"Will Harper?" Libby was confused. "How—"

"Let it go all to hell, that one did. As soon as he sniffed out that offer from the drugstore folks. Figured he didn't have to worry about keeping it up because the building was going to be knocked down anyway. That water stain…" Gwen looked over Libby's shoulder toward the dining room and her mouth puckered. "I told him from day one that Barb knew there was a leak in the bathroom upstairs. She was all set to get it fixed. You know, before the accident. And that real-estate agent, he said he'd take care of it once the building was on the market."

"And it was my responsibility to make sure he did." Not for the first time, Libby gave herself a mental kick in the pants for listening to Rick when she wanted to come take a look at the property and he advised against it. "I just didn't think—"

"That you'd ever end up here." Gwen nodded as if she understood. As if she could. Because Libby hadn't taken any tea for herself, Gwen poured some into her cup. "In case you're wondering, the front room was a delicate shade of lavender," she said. "It's looking a little gray now. And that middle room of yours, I don't know if you can tell, what with the water damage and the way those rose of Sharon on the side of the house have grown up to block the windows, but that room was the prettiest shade of yellow. I think it's the same color Barb used upstairs in her kitchen."

"You knew her well enough to visit upstairs."

"You didn't know her at all."

If Gwen had spoken the words like an accusation, Libby might have taken offense. The way it was, she couldn't be mad about something that was true. She added a dab of milk to her tea and tried to feel her way through the emotional minefield. "Was the shop successful?"

"Oh, honey!" Gwen beamed. "It was knitting heaven. Imagine all that yarn you tossed out when it was new and pretty. We had the finest selection in northeast Ohio. Mohair that would take your breath away and merino wool for sweaters and the cutest baby yarn you can imagine. And the angora…" She fanned her face with one hand. "People who don't knit wouldn't understand, but knitters…knitters can't resist yarn in any form. I remember when the boxes would arrive and I'd unpack them and just sink my hands into it all."

"And Barb, she was…" Libby wavered between blurting out the hundreds of questions she'd formulated over the years and trying to stay impersonal. It was hardly fair to bombard a complete stranger. She chose her words carefully. "Was she a good businesswoman?"

Gwen smiled. "Your mother had an uncanny knack for what customers would be looking for, even before the customers knew it themselves. And a real way with people. Talk about customer service! She was the best knitting teacher I've ever met, too, and the finest knitter." Gwen touched a hand to the tea cozy. "Take a look at this. Anybody can knit a tea cozy and anybody can grab a bunch of blue yarn and put it all together and make it look decent. But Barb, she wasn't satisfied with decent." Gwen touched a finger to a patch of violet-colored yarn that splashed across the front of the cozy like the play of sunset colors on a lake. "I never take chances when it comes to color in my knitting. Most of the knitters I know don't either. Barb, though, she had a real eye for color and she wasn't afraid to use it in ways that make you slap your forehead and wonder why you didn't think of it first."

Before she even realized she was doing it, Libby was reaching across the table. She stopped herself just in time, her finger only an inch from the cozy. It was one thing processing everything Gwen said about Barb, it was another—and a way too tangible—thing to actually make contact with something that her mother had owned.

"She made this?"

Gwen's eyes lit. "She did, and I've still got the pattern around somewhere if you want to give it a try."

Libby hid her embarrassment by taking a sip of tea. "I don't knit," she confessed. "Never have."

Gwen cocked her head. "That's not surprising, seeing that it was something Barb lived and breathed. My guess is your grandparents remembered and…well, being a grandparent myself, I know how much remembering can hurt. They associated knitting with Barb. My guess is they kept you as far from knitting as they could."

It wasn't as clear-cut as that. Libby shook her head. "Grandma P didn't knit, so there was no chance of me asking her to teach me. And besides…" She thought of the knot of yarn she'd left, along with the knitting needles that refused to obey her commands no matter how hard she tried, under the front counter. "I'm a total loser when it comes to handcrafts. My fingers don't listen to what my head tells them to do. My head can't figure out the instructions in the books. I'm not patient enough and not smart enough and—"

"And I haven't met a person yet who can't be taught to knit." Gwen gave her a wink. "Leave it to me. You'll be addicted in no time flat. Just like the rest of us."

"You mean like all the customers that used to shop here?" There was just the slightest cynicism in Libby's comment and Gwen picked up on it.

"Used to be hard finding a parking place out front, that's how busy Barb was," she said. "They came for the yarn and the lessons. They stayed because of your mother."

It was the most she'd ever heard about Barb and so incompatible with the picture Libby had formed in her head of the mindless, careless, coldhearted woman who'd forgotten her only child in a store and sold yarn from a shop that was just this side of being condemned that it left Libby confused and overwhelmed all at the same time. She blinked back unexpected tears, hiding a response she knew was illogical.

Watching Libby over the rim of her cup, Gwen sipped her tea. "Your mother talked about you all the time."

"Did she?" A single tear escaped and slipped down her cheek, and Libby wiped it away with one finger. "I didn't think she knew enough about me."

"Oh, you'd be surprised!" Gwen finished the last of her tea and took her mug to the sink to rinse it. As if she knew Libby needed the space and time to acclimate herself to this first peek into Barb's world, she didn't speak again until Libby was done with her tea.

She turned and leaned against the sink. "How's your daughter adjusting?" she asked.

Libby's laugh held no amusement at all. She set down her teacup. "Not well," she admitted. "When she's not complaining, she's sulking. And when she's not doing that, she's been up in the attic hiding out so I can't ask her to do anything."

"Or maybe she's just trying to claim a little space for herself."

Libby hadn't thought of it that way. She had to admit, the theory had merit. "She's even dragged her sleeping bag up there," she told Gwen. "I guess sharing a room with Mom isn't every teenager's dream."

"You got that right!" Gwen eyes glimmered. "Trust me, I've got four daughters of my own and I remember those teenage years like it was yesterday. Back then, my girls would have thought sharing a room with me was gross. Or *grody*."

Libby grinned. "And Meghan says it's lame."

"Not much changes." Gwen grabbed a cookie for herself and made short work of it. "Eventually she'll stop being a teenager and turn into a human being. The trick is to stay sane while she does. So…" She brushed cookie crumbs from her hands. "When are you planning on opening?"

Libby had been over the plan in her head a dozen times in the last days. Saying it out loud solidified it in her mind. It made it real. And terrifying. "School starts August twenty-seventh. That's a Wednesday. I'm thinking the Friday after.

I'm planning a soft opening and a month or so to get the kinks out, then I'll have a grand-opening celebration sometime in October. You know, an evening event, a cheese-and-wine party, that kind of thing."

Gwen nodded. "From the looks of things, you've gotten a lot accomplished, but there's a lot to do before then. What would you like me to tackle first?"

The question hit Libby out of left field, and until she found her voice, Libby could only stare at Gwen while her heart sank. Gwen was a pleasant woman. She was friendly and funny and she made killer peanut-butter cookies. Even more importantly, she was the closest thing Libby had ever come to a firsthand source of information about her mother.

All good reasons she hated to burst Gwen's bubble.

And not one of them good enough to change the fact that she had to disappoint her.

"I'm just getting started," Libby said. "I'm sure you under-stand. Thank goodness there's no mortgage on this place and that I've got my divorce settlement. But between everyday living expenses and everything I need to order for the shop, things are going to be tight around here for a while. Right now, a staff…well, it looks like it will have to be just me and Meghan for a while. At least until I've got enough cash flow to—"

"There I go again. Jumping to conclusions." Gwen didn't look as if she regretted the tendency. She reached for another cookie. "Just so you know, I don't expect to be paid," she said.

"And I wouldn't have it any other way. I couldn't possibly—"

"Sure you could!" With the hand that held the cookie, Gwen waved away Libby's concerns. Crumbs showered the floor between the sink and the table. "Number one, you're going to hear it eventually from Peg and the other neighbors so you might as well know it's true—I've got a boatload of money. Widowed twice," she explained. "And Ted and Benny, well, they were both great guys and they both had plenty to spare. Between what they left me and a rock-'em-sock-'em stock portfolio, I don't have a thing to worry about. Even when I worked for Barb I did it to keep myself busy, not for the money."

"So that's number one. And number two?"

"Ah, number two…" Gwen looked off in the distance, lost in thought. When she finally shifted her gaze back to Libby, tears added a sheen to her brown eyes. "I really miss Barb. I miss the way this place used to be. Tea parties and knitting here in the kitchen. Lessons in the classroom. We dyed wool in the backyard once. Used a big old cast-iron pot over an open fire. Smelled so bad, Peg called the fire department, and then we caught hell!" She laughed. "Not that I'm saying you should dye wool. It's messy and, yes, it is smelly. But to have even a little of that spirit back here in this place, a bit of the sense of community…well…" She cleared her throat and scooted closer to the table. "I'd like to help if you'll let me. And you'd be doing me a big favor. You'd be helping this little old lady fill her empty hours."

The idea of anyone thinking of Gwen as the stereotypical little old lady was ludicrous, and Libby laughed. That didn't mean she was about to give in.

"I'll let you help," she said and stood. "But on my terms, not yours."

"Okay, but you're not paying me."

"I'm not paying you. Yet." Libby let her words sink in before she continued. "But once we're up and going, once we're making money, then I *am* paying you. No questions asked, and no arguments or I won't let you work here at all."

"Ooh, you're a tough one. Just like your mother." The way Gwen said this, it wasn't a bad thing. "Deal." She stuck out her hand, and when Libby shook it, something told her she wasn't getting just an employee but a friend, too. "So tell me, boss, where would you like me to start?"

Libby's mind raced over the endless list. Between the cleaning and the fixing and the restocking…

She pulled in a long breath designed to settle the tension that built every time she thought about her to-do list. This time, like all those other times, the stress didn't go away. But this time—unlike all those other times—it all suddenly seemed a little more manageable.

"It's hard to know where to begin," she admitted. "There's more cleaning to do. That would be a good place to start, but I hate to make you—"

"Scrub on my hands and knees!" Gwen squealed with delight. "Remember what I said? I have four daughters. And three sons, by the way, who were the messiest critters on the face of the earth. I've washed my share of floors in my day and I still do every time the grandkids finish traipsing through the house with their skateboards and their muddy sneakers and the tadpoles they catch down by the river. Washing floors doesn't scare me. Neither does painting, just so you know. I'm hell on wheels when it comes to painting windows and woodwork."

Libby thought of the hole in the ceiling upstairs. "I don't suppose you can fix plaster, too, can you?"

The way Gwen's eyes lit up, Libby almost expected her to say she was a master plasterer, an electrician and a bricklayer to boot. Instead Gwen grinned.

"Wouldn't know a trowel from a garden shovel," she said. "Cleaning and painting are one thing. Repairs, though, that's something I always left to the men."

"Too bad. I've got a million little jobs and I could use somebody handy." She set the thought aside, and before she could invite Gwen to walk through the shop so they could decide together what needed to be done next, Gwen was already in the dining room checking out the water spot on the ceiling and shaking her head sadly.

Watching her, Libby thought of something Gwen had mentioned earlier. It was completely off topic—which was what to clean next and what to do when and how in the world she was ever going to learn to knit—but too intriguing to let go.

"Did Barb really talk about me?" she asked Gwen.

Her gaze still firmly on that water spot, Gwen crossed her arms over her chest, and Libby figured she must not have heard the question because her only response was, "If you're looking for help, there's a sort of handyman in the neighborhood. I think he'd be the perfect guy for the job."

CHAPTER 6

The "perfect guy for the job" was outside the shop the next morning when Libby stepped onto the porch to get the newspaper. He was a tall man with close-cropped silver hair and he was sitting on the front steps. He jumped up and spun around the moment the door opened, but he didn't say anything. They exchanged looks, and Libby checked out his worn jeans and Pink Floyd T-shirt. He had the sleeves rolled up and a pack of cigarettes tucked into the fold of one. There was a tattoo of a phoenix on his right bicep.

"Jesse Morrison," he said. Like the rest of him, Jesse's face was long and lean. He had high cheekbones and a jaw that was tapered and dusted with a day's growth of whiskers the color of a haystack. His chin was square, his arms were tanned and his left sneaker was worn at the toe. His right pant leg was cinched up, and he bent to smooth it into place, but not before Libby noticed the socks he was wearing. She might not know much about knitting, but she recognized handmade when she saw it, and these socks were made with small, even stitches and a great deal of skill.

Jesse didn't stick out his hand to shake Libby's until she made the first move. His fingers were long and his grip was strong, the way a man's was bound to be if he'd spent years working with his hands. "You must be Libby. Gwen told me how pretty you were."

It was a surprisingly personal thing to say, but Libby didn't take it the wrong way and Jesse's assessment of her didn't make her uncomfortable. She grinned. "Gwen didn't tell me you were a first-class bullshitter."

One corner of his mouth twitched in what was almost a smile. "She didn't say you were spot-on with reading a person, either. You look…" He scraped a finger under his nose. "You look like a lady who can use a little help."

"But not one who can be conned twice. I don't know what Gwen told you, but let's get this straight right from the get-go. If you don't let me pay you, I won't let you work."

"I've got no argument with that."

They agreed on an hourly rate that was more than Libby could afford to take out of her divorce settlement but fair nonetheless, and she stepped aside to let Jesse into the shop.

"I'm not sure exactly where to begin," she said once they were inside. Before she could even start into the list that was longer than ever thanks to the hours she'd spent fantasizing about how great it would be to have a handyman around and everything she'd have him do, Jesse was already playing with the light switch on the wall.

He flicked it up and down a couple times. Of course,

nothing happened. "Never did understand the wiring in some of these old places," he said. "I'll need to get that taken care of first. And if you're worried about code, we should switch the old fuse box to circuit breakers." He looked up at the ceiling. "Track lighting. Here." He pointed. "And here and here. What do you think? That way you can shine spotlights on the different yarns. And once we've got the wiring taken care of…" Though he must have been in his sixties, Jesse moved with the grace of an athlete. He hurried into the next room and, looking at the water spot on the ceiling, whistled long and low under his breath.

"Plaster and paint," he said, "but not before I figure out what's leaking upstairs and get that fixed. The rest of the place…"

He was already striding through, sticking his head in the classroom to check that out and heading from there into the kitchen. Libby raced to catch up.

"There's a little more cleaning out to do. I just haven't had the time." Embarrassed to show off the shop when it wasn't ready for company, she swept her arm toward the kitchen counter and the dribs and drabs she'd yet to discard. The pile included two how-to knitting books with broken bindings and pages that fell out in a steady stream, a stack of sweater patterns that were in perfectly good shape except that the styles were so outdated as to be comical and the one-eyed teddy bear.

Jesse reached for the bear. "What would you like me to do with this stuff?" he asked.

Libby's shrug said it all. She'd been going around and around with the last of the junk ever since she unearthed it. The patterns were too good to throw away and not good enough to keep. Besides, something told her as soon as she tossed them, some customer would show up looking for a pattern for a sweater with wide shoulders.

As for the rest of it…

She refused to look the bear in the eye, but even so, a prickle of recognition cannonballed through her the way it did every time she saw the stuffed toy. She warned herself against fabricating some emotional, completely illogical story to explain the feeling and decided right then and there that if she was ever going to be successful at business, she needed to get her priorities straight. And put her fantasies to rest.

"There's only so much stuff any one store can hold," she told Jesse. "You can just get rid of it all."

Jesse was as good as his word. By the time August rolled around, the wiring had been replaced, every single light in the shop worked and a series of tracks and spotlights had been added to each room. The leak in the bathroom upstairs, it turned out, was from nothing more than a poorly installed pipe beneath the sink, and once he'd fixed that and stemmed any further damage, he repaired and replastered the ceiling in the middle showroom. The loose bookshelves in the front room were remounted, the broken shelves inside the kitchen cupboards were replaced.

With the brunt of the physical labor and the remainder of the cleanup in Jesse's capable hands, Libby had time to concentrate on essentials. She established a relationship with a local bank, found an accountant and met with local newspapers and magazines to determine who could give her the best bang for her advertising buck. With an eye on her budget and her lump-sum divorce settlement, she left the ordering of yarn and supplies up to Gwen and she didn't regret her decision. While Libby worked to set up the computer she put in the one corner of the former kitchen that would be her office, she listened to Gwen on the phone with distributors, asking the kinds of questions only a knitter could ask and making the sorts of decisions Libby couldn't, not with her rudimentary knowledge of the industry.

She tried her best to absorb everything, so when Gwen ordered books, Libby listened and learned about return policies and notable knitwear designers. And when Gwen spent hours online checking out patterns and deciding which they should carry, Libby looked over her shoulder now and again and asked about which yarns they should get for the patterns and if the designers or publishers provided volume-order pricing.

When it came to buying yarn, Libby was a little more hesitant to stick her nose where it didn't belong, and Gwen understood. That didn't mean she let Libby off the hook. When the yarn reps stopped by with their samples and big books of color swatches, Gwen deftly pulled Libby into their conversations. She pointed out the differences between fingering-weight, double-knitting, worsted and bulky yarns, showed Libby how to read the care label on each skein and taught her the differences between wool and alpaca, linen and cotton, cashmere and angora and mohair.

Libby left Gwen on her own to sort through the supplies Meghan had packed away and to make long lists of what they had enough of and what they needed to order. As soon as the shop was painted, Jesse had promised to install Peg-Board along one wall in the dining room, where they could display the needles and other small essentials like crochet hooks, stitch markers and scissors. It was a wise use of space and would make finding supplies as customers asked for them a piece of cake.

It was all starting to come together.

Her white coveralls dotted with flecks of paint, Libby stretched a kink out of her back and glanced around at the shop. A few short weeks earlier she never would have imagined it could look this good. Or this clean. Then again, just a few months before she never would have dreamed she'd be the proprietor of a yarn shop.

She refused to consider the thought. Things were going well, and there was no use second-guessing the past or wishing things were different.

They weren't. They couldn't be.

End of story.

Libby dipped the roller in her hand into the tray of

lavender paint, dabbed off the excess and attacked the wall in front of her. With Gwen doing the woodwork in a nice, bright white, Jesse handling the ceilings and the cut-in around windows and doors and Libby painting the walls, they were making short order of the front room. By that evening they hoped to have a first coat on the entire first floor. The second coat would go quicker, then the Peg-Board could be put up and they could unpack and stock as the orders arrived.

Libby glanced toward the calendar she'd hung near the cash register. She'd already X'ed off half the days in August, and at the outset of the project that alone would have struck terror in her heart. With Jesse and Gwen to help her, though, the work had gone smoother than she'd anticipated and the prospect of what they had yet to accomplish wasn't nearly as frightening.

Now if only she could convince Meghan to cooperate.

As if just thinking about her daughter's sour moods and the way she disappeared up to the attic for hours at a time could make Meghan materialize, she punched through the front door with an armload of library books.

"Hey, sweetie!" Libby kept her words light. There was no use mentioning that Meghan had promised to be home an hour before. If she asked where her daughter had been, Libby knew she wouldn't get a straight answer. "You ready for lunch?"

"Nah." Meghan eyed the work they'd completed with nothing short of dismay, and Libby could well imagine why.

Each step toward reopening the shop was one more step away from Meghan's old life, and a couple long weekends with Rick and Belinda designed to allow her to reconnect with her friends back in Pittsburgh had done little to pacify her.

As young girls went, Meghan had always been one of the sweet ones. Tea parties and American Girl dolls, pink dresses and Barbie. It was the kind of childhood Libby herself had had with one big addition, the one thing Libby had always imagined and longed for: a mom who was there for her, morning, noon and night.

In spite of the pampering, the cuddling and the kind of devotion Libby had always dreamed Barb would have given her—if only Barb hadn't chosen another life—Meghan had still morphed into a teenager who was sullen and uncooperative. When she wasn't being bratty, catty and just plain annoying.

In her darker moments, Libby blamed herself. If she'd been a better wife, Rick wouldn't have walked out on her. If she was a better mother, Meghan would respond to her advice. But if she were those things, she'd be a different person, and if there was one thing Libby had learned in the months since the move to Cleveland it was that she could only be herself. It was why, that morning, she'd gone so far as to suggest that the sunflower-yellow halter top Belinda bought Meghan last time she visited wasn't appropriate for a girl Meghan's age.

And exactly the reason Meghan had decided to match it with a pair of cut-off shorts and wear it to the library.

Libby ignored that, too. Once Belinda had a child of her own, she'd understand a mother's concerns, and until then, second-guessing her fashion sense or her buying habits would only make Libby look petty.

"We're painting." Libby wasn't above stating the obvious. Not when there was the slimmest chance of drawing her daughter into the conversation. "Change your clothes and grab a brush."

"Or not."

Libby didn't have to look at Meghan. She knew a roll of the eyes went along with the comment.

"It's really not hard," she said, trying just one more time in the hopes that Meghan would relent. "And it's a good skill to have. You never know when you're going to need to paint a yarn shop."

"Yeah, like never!" Meghan plunked her books on the front counter. These days her tastes ran between graphic novels and fantasy sci-fi. She leaned back against the counter and crossed her arms over her chest. "Aren't you guys sick of working on this place?"

Before Libby could answer, Gwen did. She was finishing up the window to the left of the front door, and the smile she aimed at Meghan was sweetness itself. Which is exactly why Meghan ignored it. "Can't do a job halfway," she said. Gwen was wearing denim capris and a T-shirt that declared her World's Most Awesome Grandma. There was a spot of white paint on the tip of her nose. "We can't open if the shop isn't ready."

"That would be a shame," Meghan mumbled just loud enough to be noticed but quiet enough so she could tell Libby she'd heard wrong if her mother challenged her. "I'm going to Tanya's tonight," she said.

Tanya, a soft-spoken girl who was a couple years older than Meghan and who attended Cleveland Central Catholic, the school Meghan would be starting in a couple weeks, lived down the street. When they thought Libby wasn't around to hear, Tanya liked to talk about boys, and Meghan liked to listen. That and their age difference made Libby wary of letting the girls get too close, but so far she hadn't discouraged the friendship. Once she was in school, Meghan would meet more kids her own age. Until then, Tanya and the kids she hung around with—boys and girls from the neighborhood— were the only friends Meghan had.

But that didn't mean Libby was willing to let Meghan walk all over her.

"You mean you're *asking* if you can go to Tanya's tonight." Libby dabbed her roller into the paint tray and scrolled it across the wall the way Jesse had taught her: left and right, then up and down to distribute the paint carefully and evenly. "What are you and Tanya planning?" she asked.

"Nothing."

Libby could have answered the question herself, that's how sure she was of what Meghan would say.

"And would this nothing involve anyone else? Boys, maybe?"

"Come on, Mom!" Meghan couldn't have sounded more disgusted. She pushed off from the counter. "I'm not a little kid."

"You're my little kid." Libby stepped back and looked over her work. She touched up a strip of wall where the old paint showed through. "And I'm not going to let you go running around the neighborhood—"

"We're not going to be running around the neighborhood."

"Then I'm not going to let you not be running around the neighborhood. Not unless I know who you're with and what you're doing."

Meghan backed off. She slumped back against the front counter. "I hate being treated like a baby."

"Your mom cares about what you're doing because she loves you." The comment came from Gwen, who was moving her paint can and the newspaper on which it sat to the window nearest the counter. "That Tanya Pruitt, she's a nice girl. I know her mother. But some of those other kids…" It was Gwen's turn to roll her eyes.

"Oh, thanks. Now she'll never let me go." Meghan grabbed her books. She was headed through the doorway that led into the dining room when she was intercepted by Jesse, who had been putting the finishing touches on the ceiling in there.

"Hey, you're just in time." When Jesse didn't move, Meghan couldn't. "What do you say, kiddo. Grab a paint-brush and we'll get to work."

Other than the fact that Jesse was good at what he did and kept mostly to himself, Libby knew very little about him. What she had learned had come from Gwen, who'd told her that Jesse lived a couple streets away, he was single and he'd never been married. He wasn't a father or a grandfather, and now more than ever, it showed. Only a man who wasn't a parent would have dared a suggestion so blatant to a teenager who was just as blatantly not receptive.

Libby and Gwen exchanged looks. They knew all hell was about to break lose.

Which is why Libby was shocked when Meghan said, "All right."

"All right?" Libby looked over her shoulder and mouthed the words at Gwen, whose shrug in reply said, *Go figure*.

"I've got something for you to wear so you don't get your nice clothes all dirty." Jesse tossed a T-shirt to Meghan, who caught it in one hand, set down her books and yanked the shirt over her head. The raggy brown shirt with the words Kent State on it in fat white letters was baggy enough to hold two Meghans. It came down nearly to her knees.

"Come on." Jesse tipped his head toward the room where he'd been working. "There's a couple things you need to know before you start painting. Like how much paint to load on the brush. And how to make sure you don't make a big mess."

When Meghan and Jesse finally got down to it, Libby turned to Gwen. "Will wonders never cease?"

Gwen glanced into the dining room. "He's got a way with women, that's for sure. Always has."

It had never been the way Libby thought of Jesse. "I don't care how he does it," she said. "I'll take it for as long as it lasts."

"And for as long as it lasts... Time for a break." Gwen swiped the back of her hand across her forehead and wrapped her paintbrush in a damp paper towel. She linked one arm through Libby's. "And time for you to stop stalling."

"Me?" Because Gwen wasn't going to let go, Libby deposited her paint roller in the tray and walked toward the classroom along with her. "I haven't been stalling. Not about anything but—"

"Knitting." Gwen deposited Libby in the nearest chair. There was a pair of knitting needles on the table along with a skein of bright purple yarn. "It's time for your first lesson."

Libby swallowed hard.

"Oh, come on!" Gwen laughed and sat in the chair next to hers. "They're just knitting needles, not instruments of torture. Knitting is fun. You'll see. And it's great therapy. Don't tell me you couldn't use a little therapy."

"That's for sure. But I don't know...."

As quickly as she sat down, Gwen popped up again. "Before we get started, I'm going to get some of that iced tea we made this morning. You want some?" she asked, and when Libby said she did, Gwen went upstairs to get it from the fridge.

Left to her own devices, Libby tried to calm her suddenly pounding heartbeat by listening to Jesse as he instructed Meghan on the right—and wrong—way to paint. All the while she eyed the knitting needles on the table in front of her. They weren't the same metal needles Libby had tried— and failed miserably—to use a few weeks earlier. These needles were made of wood, and the texture and warm cocoa color made them impossible to resist. Before she could remind herself that handcrafts had never been her thing, Libby had the needles in her hands.

Just as she'd done when she tried to teach herself to knit, she made a slipknot and tucked it over the point of one of the needles. After that, she was right back where she started, staring at the yarn and the needles, feeling as if she was all thumbs and more confused than ever.

"Really?" Meghan's voice broke through Libby's concentration. "You're not kidding me, are you?"

"No way," Jesse answered. "Cross my heart. I'm serious. I knew your grandmother really well."

Grandmother? Meghan's grandmother?

Libby's head came up, but it was impossible to hear the rest of the conversation once Gwen bustled into the room with a tray of iced tea glasses and started handing them around.

What did it matter anyway?

Libby slapped the knitting needles back onto the table.

There probably wasn't anything Jesse could tell her about

Barb that Gwen already hadn't. Barb had been a fair boss and a good businesswoman. She had been a better-than-average knitter, had had a good eye for color, and customers and vendors alike praised her for having been easy to work with.

All of which said something about Barb the businesswoman, and nothing about Barb the person.

"Tea?"

Libby shook herself out of her thoughts to find Gwen standing over her, a glass of iced tea in her hands.

Libby accepted it automatically and glanced out the doorway of the classroom to where Jesse and Meghan stood side by side. Jesse was showing Meghan how to carefully apply the golden paint they'd chosen for the walls in the dining room so that it didn't splash against the woodwork that would eventually be white.

"Gwen, how do you know Jesse?"

Gwen laughed. "Jesse? Everyone around knows Jesse. He's the guy who knows how to do things, remember? Only there's one thing he can't do—can't knit worth a darn. Believe me, I know. I've seen him try. I'm not going to let you get away with the same thing. Grab those needles, girl. It's time to get down to business."

"Insert right-hand needle front to back through loop on left-hand needle." Libby chewed her lower lip as she went through the motions of knitting. While she struggled to get her hands to do what her brain advised, she held her breath.

Gwen had told her time and again that she was a tight knitter. Maybe that's why drawing the new stitch through the old one reminded her of childbirth. She grunted and pushed and finally yanked hard, and the new stitch tugged through the old one and plopped onto her right-hand needle.

It wasn't pretty. Or easy. But at least she got it done.

"A couple thousand more tries and I just might get this down pat," she told herself.

"What's that you say?" Jesse had been working out on the front porch and he came through the dining room and peeked into the classroom. He had a tool belt around his waist and a hammer in his hand. "You talking to yourself?"

"I am." Libby set her knitting on the table. It was one thing to make the needles obey when it was quiet and she could concentrate, but the least little distraction sent her mind wandering and made her knitting go kerflooey. Like it or not, in the days since she'd heard the tantalizing comment about Barb from Jesse, he had become a major distraction.

It wasn't because of what he did. Jesse was, to put it succinctly, the perfect employee. He came around early each day and he usually left late. In the hours between, he worked like a demon. His patience and skills had worked miracles. The shop looked wonderful, and when the yarn and supply shipments started to arrive as they were supposed to later that week, she was ready to stock the shelves and open the doors to paying customers. Finished with the inside of the shop, Jesse had spent the past few days weeding the postage-stamp-size plot of ground out front and planting mums he guaranteed would be blooming by the time of Libby's planned grand opening.

It wasn't what Jesse said when he was around her that toyed with Libby's mind either. Except for talking about woodworking or painting or the benefits of circuit breakers over fuse boxes, Jesse hardly said anything at all. Certainly Libby had never heard him mention Barb again.

And it wasn't as if she hadn't tried to get him to talk.

She'd asked if he'd ever been in the shop before. She'd asked how long he'd lived in the area. She'd just about come right out and told him that she'd heard what he'd said to Meghan the day they'd painted but stopped before she could. There was something uncomfortable about admitting that she'd been eavesdropping. And thinking that Meghan knew something about Barb that Libby didn't know? That was driving her crazy.

Of course, Meghan was no help at all. The one time Libby tried to broach the subject, Meghan turned her off completely. Jesse himself gave vague answers to every one of her questions, as if he was waiting for her to figure out the answers for herself.

He didn't know her well enough to suspect the truth: Libby didn't give up easily.

"You know…" She gathered up the yarn and needles and carried them along with her to the front counter. The shop wasn't very big; Jesse didn't have to move—he could still hear her. "I've been thinking of the sign outside. It's in pretty bad shape."

"I was going to ask you about that." Jesse knew better than to smoke inside the shop or anywhere near the front porch. That didn't stop him from taking a cigarette out of the package and rolling it between his fingers. "There's a guy over on West Fourteenth. Al Zelinsky. He's good with signs."

"You'll get a price for me?"

He nodded his agreement.

"Not just for repainting. I mean a totally new sign. I'm thinking about changing the name of the shop."

Was it her imagination or did Jesse freeze, his eyes narrowing the slightest bit?

The next second he was back to rolling the cigarette.

"I'm thinking of Urban Knits. Or Downtown Knits. Or maybe Metropolitan Knits. What do you think of that one? It sounds sophisticated, doesn't it? I'm looking for something, you know, something a little trendier."

His voice was as deadpan as the look he gave her. "People know it as Barb's."

"Sure. Of course. But it isn't Barb's shop anymore, and the name doesn't mean that much to me." That much was true, which hadn't kept Libby from agonizing over the decision for the past weeks. She had finally reminded herself that business success was more important than loyalty to a woman who had never earned her devotion. Barb's Knits sounded old-fashioned. Outdated. If Libby intended to reach out to the legions of young, urban knitters the industry magazines told her were just itching to spend their money, she needed to kick her image up a notch.

None of which explained why she added, "I really didn't know my mother, you know."

It was the perfect opening, and, her breath tight in her throat, she waited for Jesse to take it.

But he headed for the door and didn't say a word until he got there. "I'll get the old sign down," he said. "You decide which of those names you want. Better make up your mind before that first ad of yours is set to run."

CHAPTER 7

The first day of school for Meghan at Cleveland Central Catholic came and went without incident.

This, as far as Libby was concerned, was a good thing, and she breathed a little easier because of it. Meghan didn't say anything good about school, but she didn't say anything bad either, and for this little blessing Libby was grateful.

The first day of business for Metropolitan Knits came and went without incident, too. And without one single customer coming through the front door.

This was not so good, but though she was tempted, Libby refused to worry. The only thing she'd get from fretting over things she couldn't control was an ulcer, and besides, she didn't have time.

For the worry or for the ulcer.

Libby placed ads in local publications, joined the chamber of commerce and, so she could meet her neighbors and get involved, the local community group. The yarn and supply orders arrived, and Libby and Gwen put in long hours checking in products, sorting them and deciding how to display everything to maximum advantage.

No one was more surprised than Libby to realize that all of it—the unpacking and the pricing and displaying the merchandise—was fun.

In the past her jobs had always been clear-cut and tangible. While Rick was in law school, she worked as a file clerk in an attorney's office. And then, of course, she'd been Rick's office manager. The work was black-and-white, and while she found satisfaction in it, it was hardly creative.

And though she didn't regret a single second of it, even what she considered her real life's work—being Meghan's mother—was less imaginative than it was practical. When it came to raising a child, there were schedules to keep, reminders to be given, life skills that had to be taught and reinforced. From tooth brushing to shoe tying, homework to riding a bike, it was all important, and the surge of emotion she felt each time Meghan smiled at her—fewer and farther between these days—she'd treasure as long as she lived.

But none of it was sensual or gave Libby the same kind of pure physical joy she found sinking her hands into a ball of yarn.

Gwen had taken her ordering responsibilities seriously and she had done well. By the time the last of the boxes arrived, they had a nice variety of yarn from utilitarian wool to lightweight cotton, recycled silk to novelty yarns made with ribbon and bits of sparkle that twinkled like a million stars. The colors were nothing short of delightful, and time and again when Libby walked down into the shop in the morning and flicked on the lights, it all took her breath away.

Her first customer arrived on Saturday, the day after the shop opened, and promptly purchased three dollars and ninety-five cents' worth of stitch markers. It wasn't much of a sale, but the customer—a woman named Maureen—was pleasant and thrilled to see that what she called "her favorite knitting store" was back in business. She promised she'd mention it to the other members of her knitting guild. She also signed up for the Metropolitan Knits newsletter. If Libby ever had a mailing list of more than one name, she'd send out a schedule of classes and sales.

Fortunately by the time September was half over, Meghan had settled into a routine of school, homework and helping—begrudgingly—at the store, and the mailing list had grown to three dozen names. Libby had a small but loyal group of customers who declared her shop to be the nicest in the area and—hallelujah!—spent money on yarn and supplies and signed up for the classes Gwen would start teaching in a few more weeks.

"Three for Beginning Knitting and six for the top-down sweater class." Libby had been going over the class book and she beamed across the front counter at Gwen. "You're really pulling them in. That's terrific."

"And your knitting?" Over a stack of wool from New Zealand she was arranging on a two-tiered table, Gwen gave her a penetrating look. "How's that coming?"

Even though Gwen couldn't see Libby's knitting from

where she was standing, Libby nudged her most recent attempt farther back on the shelf under the front counter. She had tried—honest she had—but her stitches were still too tight and more often than not they popped off the needles and got lost in the tangle of yarn and the few stitches she somehow managed to complete.

"I haven't had much of a chance to practice," she told Gwen. "You know that. I've been too busy. I'm still too busy, but…" She glanced at the clock next to the cash register. "You'll be okay here by yourself tonight?"

Apparently Gwen thought her laugh answer enough. She finished stacking a particularly dreary shade of tan yarn next to orange wool and suddenly the tan yarn looked remarkably appealing. "There are some things even more important than the knit shop. Meghan is one of them. What's happening at her school is another."

"I know that." Libby did, which made her feel guilty for even thinking about anything else. It didn't mean *anything else* was going to get taken care of—unless Libby took care of it. "It's just that there's a stack of invoices to file in the office and a couple of ads for the grand opening that I need to proof and fax back and—"

"It's not going anywhere. None of it! You, however, are. Meet the Teacher Night starts at seven, doesn't it?" It wasn't until Gwen stared at her that Libby finally got the message. She had to get moving if she had any hopes of getting across town in time.

She scurried out from behind the counter and headed for the door. "Meghan's upstairs doing her homework," she said. "I reminded her that we're open until eight tonight and told her that when she's done with her algebra she should come down and see if you need any help."

"I won't."

This was not as comforting a statement as Gwen had hoped. If she didn't need any help, it meant there weren't any customers. And if there weren't any customers—

As she had so many times in the last weeks, Libby automatically looked out the front window to see if any cars had pulled up outside. Except for a couple kids on their skateboards, the street was empty. Like it or not, every doubt Libby had ever had about the shop being a success came rushing back at her, right along with the words she'd heard from Rick so many times after she'd announced she was coming to Cleveland. The ones about how uprooting Meghan's life to follow some half-assed business venture and a dream of finding out more about her mother was nothing short of selfish, not to mention pathetic.

Libby shook her doubts aside and reminded Rick's voice that she didn't need to, want to, have to listen to him anymore.

"If you need me, I've got my cell phone," Libby told Gwen. "And if Lois comes in—you remember her, she's the one who ordered the pink baby yarn with the little nubs of white and yellow in it—it's all packed and under the counter. She gave me a twenty-dollar deposit, so she owes us—"

"You're acting like a new mother who's leaving her baby with a sitter for the first time!" Gwen grinned and put an arm around Libby's shoulders for a brief hug. "Relax, honey. I know the drill. And I know Lois. And the yarn she ordered. And—" When Libby opened her mouth, Gwen stopped her. "I know about Meghan's homework, so you don't have to tell me again. Meghan and I will be fine. You will be, too, but not if you don't get moving. Go." She gave Libby a little push toward the door. "Have a good time."

Libby remembered a time when the prospect wouldn't have seemed so remote. Back in Cranberry, she knew the other parents at Meghan's school and the other parents knew her. The first school function of the year was always a time to catch up on summer events and touch base about the school year, what was planned and who was taking charge of what committee.

Tonight, making the crosstown trip to a school she'd only set foot in once when she'd registered Meghan to talk to teachers she'd never laid eyes on before and who didn't have any sort of history with her daughter and to meet parents who wouldn't know Libby if they tripped over her...

Libby drew in a breath.

"I am a little stressed about this, huh?" She tried for a laugh that fell flat against her insecurities. "I just wish the teachers knew Meghan better. Then I might have more to say to them. They need to know that she doesn't always stay focused on her work. And if they don't know she's reading well above her grade level, they might think she's goofing off when everyone's still reading and Meghan's done. They need to know that, too."

"They will know it. It's a good school, and they're not going to let Meghan slip through the cracks. Besides, you'll make sure they find out everything they need to know. But not if you miss the event altogether."

It was the final push Libby needed. She opened the door to walk outside.

And immediately stepped back into the shop.

"It's freezing out there. When did it get so cold?"

Libby supposed the look Gwen gave her meant that if she'd get her nose out of the store once in a while she would have realized the temperature had dipped.

Not knowing what to expect from the school, the teachers or the other parents in attendance, Libby had dressed conservatively for Meet the Teacher Night. She'd chosen a black pantsuit and a white blouse, then decided someone might mistake her for one of the nuns who taught at Central Catholic and changed to a cream-colored shirt. The outfit was simple, basic and hardly warm enough.

"I've got to zip upstairs for a jacket," she told Gwen. "While I'm up there, I can check on Meghan and see how she's doing. You don't know anything about algebraic equations, do you? Because I'm not all that good at math and—"

"You're doing it again." Gwen's look was as straight to the

point as her words. One hand out, palm flat, she instructed Libby to stay put and headed into the classroom. That morning, she'd brought in a box of her own knitted garments so they would have some sweaters, scarves and socks to display in the store to show customers what they could accomplish with the right yarn and a little guidance. She rummaged through it all, her voice raised so that Libby could hear.

"You're dragging your feet because you're afraid to get over to that school. What are you worried about, honey? What they're going to say about Meghan? Or how going to a school function without your ex means you're the one in charge now?"

Libby thought about arguing, but it was hard to debate the truth.

"Both," she said. "What if Meghan isn't doing well? What if her work isn't up to par or if she's not making friends? What am I going to do?"

"You're going to do exactly what you would have done before that son-of-a-bitch ex of yours pulled your self-esteem out from under you." Gwen came back into the front room, something white and lacy draped over one arm. "You're going to call the girl's father. You're going to discuss any problems she might be having. Then you're going to handle it. Here." She passed the soft white article to Libby. "Toss this around your shoulders. I know— It looks too light to be warm. But, trust me, it's mohair, and if it can keep those mountain goats who grow it warm, it can keep you nice and toasty, too."

Libby unfolded the knitting and held it at arm's length. It was a rectangular shawl made with large needles and fine, fuzzy yarn the color of new-fallen snow. Every once in a while there was a slub of mauve or a thread of silver in it. The pattern of stitches reminded Libby of a fan, and the result was a gossamer cobweb so simple yet as beautiful as anything Libby had ever seen. She was a new enough knitter to be impressed.

When Gwen took the shawl out of her hands and wrapped it around her shoulders, Libby rubbed her cheek against the fuzzy yarn.

"There." Gwen grinned. "Now you don't look so much like a nun."

"The cream-colored shirt didn't do it, huh?" Libby laughed. She wrapped her arms around herself. The shawl was large and so comfortable she felt as if she were wrapped in a hug. "It's gorgeous."

"It ought to be. Your mother made it."

Libby stopped just as she was about to stroke the yarn. "I'd better get a move on," she told Gwen, and before Gwen could ask—and before Libby could examine her own feelings enough to think about why wearing her mother's shawl made her feel warm on the outside and incredibly lonely within—she hurried out to Meet the Teacher Night.

"Mrs. Cartwright? May I speak with you for a moment, please?"

Like Meghan, Libby had attended a private Catholic high

school, and old habits died hard. Apparently the knee-jerk reaction that resulted from being called to the front of the room by a nun was one of the hardest to break.

A surge of jitters shot through Libby when Sister Mary Francis waved her out of the line of parents waiting to walk out of homeroom. They were following an abbreviated version of their children's schedules, and now that the first bell had rung, she was supposed to be heading for Meghan's first-period algebra class.

Instead, her heart in her throat, Libby stepped toward the desk and the nun waiting for her.

"My dog ate my homework." Libby was hoping for funny.

Sister Mary Francis barely smiled. "There's not a lot of time at a function like this," she said, and much to Libby's horror, she realized she and the nun were dressed in the identical outfit. Except for the shawl, of course. Libby held it a little tighter around her shoulders. Partly to reassure herself that she was not a complete idiot when it came to style. Mostly in the hopes that no one would notice she and Sister Mary Francis were twins. At the same time, Sister touched a hand to the day planner on her desk. "I wondered if we could set up a meeting. To talk about Meghan."

Libby's own nervousness—not to mention the ultimate in fashion faux pas—was forgotten beneath a rush of concern. "She's in trouble?"

"No, no. Nothing like that." Sister's fleeting smile wasn't convincing. "Not yet anyway. But she's been late. Once this week. And once…" She checked a computer printout on her desk. "And once last week. She takes the bus to school?"

Libby thought of the confusion of city bus routes. One bus downtown, a transfer there and then a different bus to school. It was too much to ask of a child who'd just moved to the area. She shook her head. "I drive her."

Sister pursed her lips. "You should stop in at the office when you're late. That way the attendance secretary will know Meghan has a legitimate excuse."

"Only she doesn't." It was Libby's turn to try for a half smile. "An excuse, that is," she explained. "We've been on time every day. I've made sure of it. If she's been coming in late—"

"She's going somewhere after you drop her off." Sister's look said it all. "You can stop in next week?" She didn't wait for Libby to answer, just grabbed a pen and checked her planner. "Tuesday would be good. Around four. It would certainly reinforce the importance of our meeting to Meghan if your husband could make it, too."

It wouldn't be the last time someone assumed Meghan was from a traditional home with a traditional mom-and-dad support system.

But it was the first.

Libby swallowed down the sudden knot in her throat. "No dad," she said. "At least not here in Cleveland. Just me. As for next week…" She thought of the yarn rep who was supposed to stop in at the store the next Tuesday. She and Jesse were scheduled to visit Al Zelinsky and look at a mock-up of the store's new sign that same day. "I'll be here," she said at the same time another bell rang and she realized she was late for Meghan's first class.

"Do I need a hall pass?" she asked

Sister's stony expression said it all.

By the time Libby found her way to algebra, the teacher was already showing the textbook to the parents, who were squeezed into desks that were far too small for adults. She slipped into the desk nearest the door, and for once she was grateful to be short; her knees didn't knock into the desk in front of her.

"I was hoping you'd show up here." A woman about Libby's age with long blond hair and a wide smile whispered across the aisle. "I saw you in homeroom and I was wondering…"

The teacher—a bland-looking man named Mr. McCarthy—stopped talking and looked in their direction. The woman clammed up.

Mr. McCarthy started into his lecture again and the woman pointed toward Libby. "About that."

It took Libby a minute to realize the woman was talking about her shawl, but by that time it was too late to continue the conversation. Mr. McCarthy was explaining his homework policy, and Libby didn't want to miss a word.

She was still wondering why the woman cared about the shawl when the period ended.

"It's fabulous." The woman introduced herself as Susan

Barker. "I'm a knitter." Susan said this in a matter-of-fact way that made Libby wonder how anyone could admit to a skill so baffling with such nonchalance. "Well, a new knitter. But I can tell the good stuff when I see it." She didn't seem embarrassed to be forward enough to check out the stitches and the yarn. "This is gorgeous. You must really know what you're doing. How long have you been knitting?"

Libby felt heat color her cheeks while she debated the best way to answer. *I don't know how to knit and, oh, yeah, by the way, I own a knit shop* struck her as a little too honest, so she decided on an answer that wasn't exactly an answer and hoped Susan wouldn't notice.

"My mother made the shawl," she said. "She owned a shop over in the Tremont neighborhood. I'm running it now."

"A knitting store?" Susan practically swooned. "Talk about dying and going to heaven! I hope you've got this yarn in stock. I might only know how to do garter stitch, but with yarn like that even plain ol' garter stitch would look spectacular."

Fortunately Libby had been paying attention to Gwen's instruction and knew what Susan was talking about. Garter stitch was what she was learning. Or at least what she was trying to learn. Garter stitch was created simply by knitting every row. "We've got lots of yarn," she told Susan, smoothly avoiding the question about this particular yarn while making a mental note to order it. "And we're teaching classes, too. And—"

"Cecilia! Angela!" By this time they had stepped into the

hallway to head to the next class, and Susan called to two moms who were headed toward the nearby stairway. "Take a look at this. She owns a yarn shop. This is—"

"Libby." Libby provided the information and dug in her purse for the business cards she'd been smart enough to tuck inside. She handed one each to Angela, Cecilia and Susan. "I hope you'll stop in," she told the ladies. "We've got a great selection."

"And classes," Susan chimed in. "Angela and I took a beginner's class together. You know, at one of those big-box craft stores. We've got the basics down but they're not very good when it comes to answering questions, and we can't make scarves for the rest of our lives." She glanced at Libby's card, then at her friends. "What do you say? We'll go over this Saturday and sign up for more classes?"

"I want to make sweaters," Angela said. "I know that's crazy. I mean, you must have to be a really good knitter to even attempt something like that."

"Not really." Things she'd heard Gwen say came rushing back at Libby and she was glad. "Think about a drop-shoulder sweater." She demonstrated, her hands in the air. "It's really just two rectangles. One for the front and one for the back. With two triangles—one for each sleeve."

Before she could lower her arms again, Cecilia caught hold of one side of the shawl. "If you could teach me to make something this beautiful, I'd do them as Christmas presents."

"Absolutely." Libby hoped the pattern was still around

somewhere. "We've got some mohair that would be perfect. It's lightweight but plenty warm. Hey, if it can keep the mountain goats who grow it cozy through the winter…" She listened to her words echo what Gwen had said earlier in the evening and laughed. "Stop by. We'll make a pot of tea and you can look around the shop."

The ladies said they would and the bell rang. Too bad. No one was more surprised than Libby to realize she was enjoying herself. She could have gone right on talking about fiber and colors and the latest trends in knitwear. Unfortunately she had to get to English class.

"You're still knitting too tight. Breathe, girl! It's not brain surgery."

Libby struggled to poke the tip of the right-hand needle into the stitch on the left-hand needle. All she managed to do was somehow slide three stitches off the left needle completely. The stitches slipped down one row, then the next, and all her hard work unraveled before her eyes.

"You're right. It's not brain surgery. It's harder than that!" Libby tossed her needles—and the mess on them that would never pass for knitting—down on the table in the classroom. "I give up."

"You can't. I won't let you."

Being bossed around by a feisty senior citizen wasn't about to change Libby's mind. Even when the senior citizen in question was dressed in a navy-blue power suit in honor of an appointment with her financial planner later that morning.

Libby crossed her arms over her chest. "No more knitting. I don't need to knit. I have you to do that."

"And if folks come in and ask questions?"

"You'll answer them."

"And if they want advice?"

"You'll give it to them."

"And when they want you to teach them a stitch?"

The prospect was too terrifying to even consider.

Libby pushed back from the table and stood. "You can teach all the classes. Just as you are now. I'll run the business end of the shop. That way I'll never have to show anybody anything."

"And when I head off to the south of France for eight weeks after Christmas, the way I do every winter?"

Libby's eyes widened with horror. Her heart jumped into her throat.

At least until Gwen started to laugh.

"Got you there, sweetie!" Gwen patted the seat of the chair Libby had just vacated. "Come on and sit back down. I'm not going to the south of France. Honest! I've never been to the south of France. I have no desire to go to the south of France. All I want to do is show you how to knit."

"You've tried. It's not working."

"It's not going to work if you don't keep at it." Gwen reached for her own knitting and talked while she worked.

Her stitches were neat and all the same size and they didn't drop off the needles and unscramble themselves. The edges of the triangular shawl she was working on were nice and even. There weren't any lumps in her work. No holes or tangles or knots. "And don't be so sure you can hide behind the cash register and avoid customers with questions." She glanced at Libby and kept working, her fingers dancing a smooth rhythm. "Now that you've got every mother at Cleveland Central Catholic storming the place, sooner or later you're bound to run into a knitter who needs help when I'm not around."

Gwen was right. About the inevitability of being called on the knitting carpet, so to speak, and about the sensation she'd created at Meghan's school.

One prospect was terrifying to say the least.

The other helped her sleep easier at night.

"Imagine, one little shawl..." Libby didn't need to explain; Gwen knew exactly what she was talking about. Ever since Meet the Teacher Night, word had gone around school about the shop, the yarn and the shawl. The knitters at Central Catholic told their knitter friends. Their knitter friends belonged to knitting guilds and knitting clubs, and thanks to them, word of a new shop spread like wildfire. Suddenly it seemed as if every knitter within a fifty-mile radius wanted to duplicate the shawl.

It was now two weeks later, a Wednesday, and just a little after nine in the morning. The shop didn't open until ten, so it was still early for the customers who had been arriving in a steady stream since the night Libby wore Barb's shawl to school.

She was relieved not to have to pace the store, looking out the window and waiting for customers who never came. She was grateful that the knitters who had discovered Metropolitan Knits were willing to spend their hard-earned dollars on yarn and supplies. Heck, she was thrilled. Finally the shop was creating a sensation and making a name for itself within the community of Cleveland knitters.

What she wasn't was convinced she could ever be one of them.

"I don't have the knitting gene," she grumbled.

"Ridiculous." When Gwen patted the chair again, there wasn't much Libby could do other than sit down. Or run away and hide.

She sat down.

"No daughter of Barb Palmer's can possibly be incapable of knitting. It's statistically impossible," Gwen said. She set her knitting down and reached across the table for a skein of yarn. It was a soft, beautiful merino wool in a shade of gray that reminded Libby of the slate-colored water of Lake Erie this time of year. There was another skein nearby, a composite yarn in shades of pink from the softest baby color to hot, hot, hot. It was formed from three strands: one made up of long, wispy hairs, one metallic and one studded with blobs of twisted fibers that reminded Libby of pearls on a string. It was one of the most expensive yarns the shop carried, and because she'd been convinced nobody would pay that kind of money for yarn, Libby had been reluctant to order it. Once it had arrived, though, and she'd seen how gorgeous it was, she was glad she had it in stock—and anxious for customers to discover it.

"Maybe we're just not approaching this the right way," Gwen said. She slid the glitzy pink yarn toward Libby. "We've been practicing with cheap yarn."

"Yeah. For a reason. Cheap yarn isn't expensive. That means that when I end up throwing away my knitting, it doesn't cost me as much."

"And I can't fault you for being careful with your stock." There was another skein of the same kind of yarn nearby, this one in shades of green, and Gwen grabbed it and took two sets of fat wooden needles out of the old dresser where they stored class supplies. "Cast on thirty-six stitches," she instructed.

Libby was not convinced. "Thirty-seven bucks a hank," she said, turning the tag on the fancy yarn over so Gwen could see it even though she was sure Gwen already knew how much it cost. "We mark most things up one hundred percent. That means I paid—"

"Whatever!" Gwen dismissed Libby's concern in a tone of voice that reminded Libby a whole lot of Meghan. "Here's what I think. You've been practicing with okay yarn, and that's all well and good. But you're more likely to want to learn to knit if there's a carrot at the end of the stick."

"We're knitting carrots?"

"We're knitting shawls. Like Barb's shawl only with a little more pizzazz. Grab one end of both the yarns—the merino and the glitzy stuff—and cast on thirty-six stitches," she said again, and Gwen did just that and waited for Libby to catch up.

"Now we're going to knit across the whole first row. You'll have to be careful. That fancy stuff tangles easily."

"And this is supposed to make me feel better about knitting?"

"Give it some time. Look how every stitch you do looks a little different. The wool gives your shawl body and warmth. But the other stuff…" Gwen jiggled her shoulders. "Oh, kid, in that you're going to be one hot little number."

Libby wasn't so sure. "I think my hot-number days are over," she said and she did another few stitches. By the time she got to the end of the row her fingers ached because she was so tense, but all thirty-six stitches were exactly where they were supposed to be.

She breathed a sigh of relief.

"Don't get bigheaded." Gwen poked her in the ribs with her elbow. "Now we'll do the same for the next row, but we're going to add a little something. Instead of just knitting, we're going to do some fancy stuff. We'll yarn over…" She did this as she talked. "Then knit two together." She did that, too.

Even before she made an effort to follow Gwen's lead, Libby's head was spinning. The yarn over involved nothing more than bringing the working yarn from the back of the needles to the front, then knitting as usual. *That* she could handle.

Knitting two together, however…

Gwen made it look easy. Thanks to her tight stitches, her nervousness and her sweaty hands, Libby found it anything but.

"Keep trying." Gwen zipped through a row and started another one, smoothly slipping the yarn-over stitches from the left needle and letting them fall to form a long, flowing stitch. "And don't get discouraged. Haven't seen anyone yet who can't knit when they put their mind to it."

"And if I don't put my mind to it?"

The older woman laughed. "You will. You'll see. I remember what your mother used to tell her knitting students. 'Just wait,' she'd say. 'One day it will come to you in a flash and after that you'll be hooked. A knitting addict like the rest of us.'"

They'd been so busy with the store, customers and planning the grand opening, they hadn't had much time to talk about Barb. Libby used this opportunity to dig for more information. If she wasn't going to get it from Jesse, perhaps Gwen could tell her something.

"Does Jesse knit?" she asked.

Gwen pursed her lips. "Seen him try."

"Did my mother teach him?"

The look Gwen gave her was fleeting but perceptive nonetheless. "Yes, Barb was the one who tried to teach him."

"So he's been here before?"

Gwen finished a row, turned her work and started a new row. "I guess he must have been," she said.

"Did he know my mother well?"

Gwen's fingers stilled over her work. She stared at her knitting, fixed what was apparently a mistake, then went on. "What's Jesse said about it?" she asked.

Libby wasn't about to lie. "Not a thing. I've tried to get him to open up, but—"

"If he's not talking, then why should I?" Gwen scraped her chair back and stood. She'd left her purse on the floor and she reached for it and slung it over her shoulder. "There's a new student stopping in this morning, remember. Private lessons. Beginning Knitting."

It wasn't in the class book, but Libby didn't question it. If Gwen wanted to accept private students who paid more than the students who took group lessons, it was fine with her. "What time?" she asked.

Gwen checked her watch. "I'd say another fifteen minutes or so."

"You're cruel." Libby could afford to say it with a light tone. Gwen was teasing her again. "You told me you were leaving for your appointment with your financial planner at ten. And if the student's coming in at ten—"

"You got that right."

"But how are you going to teach a class when you're not here?"

It was a bona fide question and it deserved an honest answer.

Which didn't explain why Gwen laughed and headed for the door. "Your mother always said it best, honey. She said, 'Teaching provides the best learning.'"

"And that means…?"

"It means you're going to teach the class."

"But I don't know how to knit!"

"Oh, you will. Don't worry about it. By the time the morning is over I guarantee you'll be a better knitter than you are right now."

"But—" Libby knew there was no use arguing. And what good would it have done her anyway? Gwen had made up her mind and nothing was going to change it. Besides, even if Libby wanted to protest, she knew she didn't have time. As soon as Gwen was out the door, she scurried into the front room to grab every book she could about knitting technique. Maybe if she crammed, she could pack some knowledge into her head before her student arrived.

Twenty minutes later she was bent over a book at the counter next to the cash register when the front door opened. Anxiety overwhelmed her and Libby's heart pounded.

It settled down again when she looked up and saw a man standing just inside the door.

She had a reprieve.

"You're lost." It was the most natural thing to assume. After sixteen years of marriage, she knew how much guys hated to ask for directions. "You're looking for the freeway. Or maybe Lincoln Park. That's easy. Right across the street."

The man was forty or so, a smidgen under six feet tall, with sandy hair a little too long and thick enough to curl at the shirt collar that showed from beneath his heavy cream-colored fisherman knit sweater. He wasn't as big as he was simply broad, a powerful man with large hands and large square fingers.

Not Libby's type, and just having the thought surprised her. So did the fact that, type or not, she felt suddenly self-conscious under the man's very level gaze. And all too aware that it had been a long time since she'd had sex.

Afraid something in her eyes might give her away—and that she'd be embarrassed to death because of it—Libby flipped closed the book she was reading and shuttered her feelings at the same time she warned her hormones to shut up and behave. Rather than risk the man thinking she was rude or, worse, a poor businesswoman, she forced herself to meet his gaze.

His eyes were blue, a shade too delicate for a man with such a powerful build. His smile didn't seem to fit either. It wavered around the edges, as if something about being inside a shop that traditionally catered to women made him uncomfortable.

"Not lost," he said. "Though I have to admit, I thought about getting lost a couple times on my way over here. You know, purposely. I'm Hal. Hal O'Connor."

"And I'm Libby. But I'm afraid I don't know—"

"She didn't tell you, did she?" Hal laughed. It was a deep

sound that, like his smile, made Libby think he was feeling self-conscious.

"I talked to Gwen yesterday," Hal said. "She told me she wouldn't be around today, but she did mention that you'd be here. So here I am, as ready as I'll ever be. I'm putting myself in your capable hands. You see, I'm your new knitting student."

CHAPTER 8

"**I**'m not gay, you know."

Hal's comment came just after Libby had settled him at the table in the classroom and right as she was retrieving two balls of the worsted yarn they would use for practice. Whether he was gay or not wasn't something she'd thought of—at least not that she was willing to admit. Thinking how glad she was to hear the news—and wondering why it mattered—she fumbled the yarn. Both balls would have hit the floor if Hal wasn't quick enough to scoop them out of the air with his left hand.

"Just thought we should get that out in the open so you don't get the wrong impression." He handed the yarn back to her. "I know it's a stereotype and probably not politically correct, but let's face it, how many straight guys do you know who knit?"

Libby didn't even bother to try to answer.

She was too nervous about trying to teach anyone to knit—especially when the *anyone* in question was the first man she'd met in what felt like forever who made her remember that she was a woman with wants and needs that went beyond school uniforms and knitting worsted. It was crazy to respond to a complete stranger so strongly, so quickly or with the kind of physical awareness she hadn't felt in years, and so unlike Libby it scared her half to death.

Fortunately Hal didn't wait for her to formulate a response. "I guess some shrink would put a different spin on it. You know, since I came out and said I'm heterosexual, it shows that I'm insecure and not comfortable with my own sexuality." When he looked her way, a smile played around the corners of his mouth. "I'm willing to take that chance. I wouldn't want a pretty woman to get the wrong idea about me."

Libby nearly asked which pretty woman he was talking about.

She gave herself a mental slap. Was she so pathetic that she'd forgotten what flirting was like?

Okay, not so pathetic but so not ready to go there. From a personal—or a professional—point of view.

She reminded herself not to forget it.

"You mean you think someone will assume you're gay because you want to learn to knit."

He leaned back. His chair creaked. "That's the thing, see. I mean, I don't exactly *want* to learn to knit. I guess Gwen didn't explain that either."

"She didn't." Libby moved her knitting and Gwen's from the table and set it on an empty chair. When she thought Hal wasn't looking, she took a quick look at the label on the yarn they'd be using. The manufacturer suggested size-eight needles. Who was she to argue? She took two sets of needles from the store stash and handed needles and vibrant blue yarn to Hal. When she sat down with her own supplies, she whispered a silent prayer.

If there was a knitting god, now would be a very good time for him—or her—to show a little compassion toward a non-knitter who'd been conscripted into teaching a skill she did not personally possess. Or understand.

Divine support would sure come in handy.

A miracle wouldn't hurt either.

For now, she'd settle for a little time to compose herself and maybe figure out what her next move should be. In regards to knitting, of course.

There didn't seem to be a better way to accomplish that than by stalling.

"So you're here because you don't want to be here." Libby nodded sagely and hoped her strategy wasn't too transparent. Gay or straight, excited about learning to knit or not, Hal was a paying student. She couldn't afford to come across as too nosy, unprofessional or so obviously unprepared to teach that she was making small talk to pass the time.

Even though she was.

Thankfully, he was not one of those obtuse types to stare at her, confused. His nod mirrored hers. "Right you are," he said. "I'm here because my therapists say I have to be here."

"Those shrinks you mentioned earlier?"

"Not those kind of therapists." Now that he'd gotten the

I'm-not-gay part of the conversation out of the way, Hal's smile was easier and more relaxed. "Physical therapists. Occupational therapists. Massage therapists. You name the therapist and I've got at least one."

"And they say you have to learn to knit?"

"They say I have to increase my dexterity." Hal slowly flexed his right hand, and for the first time Libby noticed the scar that slashed his palm from just above his wrist all the way to the base of his middle finger. It wasn't a small, clean scar like the kind that results from surgery. This scar was thick and angry-looking, still tinged with red and so smooth and tight she imagined every movement must have been excruciating. The ring finger of the same hand was misshapen, too, slanted toward the little finger at an unnatural angle from the knuckle up.

Before she realized she was doing it, she was leaning over his hand. "You were injured," she said, and heat spread up her neck. "I'm sorry. It's none of my business. I'm afraid it's the mother in me."

"I'm not complaining. It's kind of nice to have a woman worry about me." The way he said it made Libby sit back in her chair. It was that—and moving out of the pull of that magnetic little rumble in his voice—or risk being sucked in forever.

She dared a tiny smile and felt like an idiot for it. There must be a neon sign flashing *Lame!* above her head in letters as bright and as red as she knew her cheeks must be. "No other woman is worried about you?"

Hal's smile inched up a notch. Maybe he didn't notice the sign. "Not at this particular moment," he said. "Not one particular woman anyway." His eyes glittered. "Right now I've got six women in my life."

"Six!"

He'd gotten the reaction he wanted and Hal laughed. "Boats," he said, and Libby caught on.

"Boats are always referred to as *her* and *she*."

"Yes, ma'am." He appreciated not having to explain. "And right now there are six of them sitting in my shop in various stages of completion and customers who have been waiting since the middle of June. Thanks to my hand, I can't work on any of those boats. My customers expect me to be in on every phase of the building, not sitting on the sidelines. I'd like to show them at least some progress."

"June—that's when you got hurt?"

He nodded. "Had a winch slip and a motor come down…." He shrugged as if it was no big deal and went right on talking. "They said I'd never use my hand again. But, hell, I'm not going to let a couple orthopedic surgeons stop me. What do those guys know anyway? But now they've got me between a rock and a hard place. They won't give me the okay to return to work until I prove I can use my hand without too much trouble. And without their okay, my insurance company won't cover me for anything down at the shop. The therapists suggested one of the ways I could build up my hand muscles was—"

"Knitting."

They finished with the same word at the same time and exchanged smiles.

"Well, I can't say much for the medical efficacy of knitting." That was an understatement if Libby ever heard one. She couldn't say much of anything about knitting. Not with any authority at least. "But Gwen always says knitting is good therapy. Only I don't think she means physical therapy."

"And why would a woman like you need any other kind?"

It was tempting to answer with the whole truth and nothing but. Which was exactly why Libby knew it was a bad idea.

"Let's get started," she said instead and she grabbed the yellow yarn she'd taken out for herself and showed Hal how to find the end of the yarn that pulled from the middle of the ball. That was the easy part and the only one she felt comfortable demonstrating. It took maybe five seconds. One hour, fifty-eight minutes and fifty-five seconds of class time to go.

"Slipknot." The word whooshed out of Libby at the end of a nervous little breath. She congratulated herself. She'd remembered the next step without too much trouble, and this one should take a little longer. She knew that often beginning knitters had trouble with the pretzel-like configuration that resulted in a slipknot.

Of course, none of them were boatbuilders.

Sore hand or not, Hal had a slipknot on the end of one needle in no time flat.

It took Libby a little longer, but once her slipknot—the first crucial stitch—was in place, she felt better. But just a little.

"Now you're all set for what's called casting on," she told him. She scrambled to remember everything she'd heard Gwen say to her students and congratulated herself when it came out sounding as though she knew what she was talking about. "Every knitted piece has to start with casting on because that's how you get the first row of stitches on your needles. How many stitches you cast on usually depends on how wide you want something to be. You'll see casting on abbreviated in patterns as CO. Only…" She grimaced, and though she'd been on something of a roll, her confidence evaporated when she realized she'd been repeating Gwen's words by rote and had forgotten that Hal's circumstances were special. "I guess you're not planning on ever knitting anything from a pattern, are you?"

"Not unless it's a big ole billboard that says, *Hey, doctors, look! I can use my hand again.* Any chance of knitting something like that?"

Libby took the question at face value. Thinking hard and seeing another way to put off the inevitability of the rest of the lesson, she wrinkled her nose. "I think I did see something in one of the books up front about knitting initials on sweaters. If you can knit initials, I don't see why you can't knit words. I could find the book and—"

When she made a move to get up, Hal stopped her. "I was only kidding," he said. "I don't want to knit a billboard. I don't want to knit anything. I just want to get my hand moving again."

"Oh." Libby settled back in her chair. "Of course." The smile she gave him was as tight as she knew her stitches would be. "Then I guess I need to show you how to cast on."

Because it was easier to show him than it was to explain, she demonstrated. She took one end of the yarn and put it over her index finger. The other end she draped over her thumb. So far, so good. Panic kick-started her brain and automatically her fingers went through the motions.

"Needle down this way," she said, pulling the needle toward her wrist. "Then this way and—"

Instead of having a second stitch on her right needle, the way Gwen always did, she ended up with a tangle of yarn.

"Let me try that again," she said. She went through the steps again. And this time...

"Success!" The second stitch on her right-hand needle where it belonged, Libby grinned and breathed a huge sigh of relief. "You cast on as many stitches as you need," she said, sounding far more pleased with herself than she had any right to be. "And then you can start knitting. That's all there is to it."

It was Hal's turn to nod, but he didn't follow her lead. Instead he looked her in the eye. "That's not all there is to it," he said. "You're leaving out one important part."

"I am?" Libby flipped through her mental Rolodex of knitting facts, but the harder she tried to remember what she'd forgotten, the more flustered she got. And the more flustered she got, the more sure she was that Hal would know she was a fraud.

She swallowed hard. "You must have tried knitting before, otherwise you wouldn't know that I'd forgotten something."

"Nope." He sat back in his chair, his head cocked, and studied her. "Don't have to be a knitter to see what's going on here. I know exactly what you forgot to tell me."

She was almost afraid to ask. "What?"

A smile dissolved his serious expression. "You have no idea what the hell you're doing, do you?"

It was Hal's candor—and that he was such a good sport— that put Libby at ease. By the time she confessed that he was absolutely right about her lack of skills, that she was absolutely embarrassed to admit it and that she absolutely, positively had to refer to one of the how-to books if she had any hopes of getting them through the next two hours, they were both laughing. They sat side by side, the book open in front of them and their heads together, going through the motions of casting on, then doing the knit stitch and congratulating each other on their small success.

She could tell that Hal's hand hurt, but she also knew that wasn't going to stop him. He paused once in a while to flex his fingers or rest his hand, but he kept right on, and his determination redoubled her own. In what felt like no time at all, they each had a few rows of knitting on their needles.

Hal's stitches were loose and loopy, which was no surprise. He could barely close his hand around the right needle, and his fingers were stiff and often unresponsive.

For once, Libby's stitches weren't firm enough to double as chain mail and not so tight that it looked as if her needles might snap in two. This was a good thing, she told herself, and while she tried to credit her success to experience, she wondered if being with Hal had anything to do with the transformation.

Silly, she told herself.

Illogical.

But for the first time in what felt like a very long time, it dawned on her that she wasn't worried about cash flow or projected sales or if the current knitting craze would keep up long enough so that the revenues from Metropolitan Knits would help put Meghan through college. She was having a good time.

Was there something to this knitting therapy after all?

Maybe, but Hal didn't seem to know it. A twinge of pain creased one corner of his mouth and he set his needles on the table. He massaged his right palm with this left thumb.

Far be it from Libby to be too bold, but it was easy to see that none of this was easy for him. Knitting with two good hands was hard enough. "Hurts, huh?"

"Like the devil." He wasn't happy to admit it.

"We could stop."

"Yeah. But I'd like to do a couple more rows. You know, so I don't forget. That way I can practice until our next class."

She didn't hesitate to make the offer she would have made to any student. "If you forget, you can always stop in. We'll be happy to show you—"

Still rubbing his hand, he smiled at her. "Is that an invitation?"

Libby had been so busy worrying about her knitting she'd almost forgotten the punch his smile packed. Almost.

A prickle of heat shot through her. "Not what I meant," she told him. But though the words were right, the breathiness of her voice betrayed her. "Gwen is usually here and—"

"How about you? If I stop in, will you be here?"

She didn't have a chance to answer. It had been a quiet morning, and the sound of the front door slamming startled Libby. She spun around.

Meghan was just walking through the middle showroom, her backpack slung over one shoulder. She took one look at Libby, another at Hal and stopped cold, her eyes narrowed with something that looked a whole lot like suspicion.

Until she saw the look in Meghan's eyes, Libby hadn't even realized she'd leaned closer to Hal in response to his voice. Even though she had nothing to feel guilty about, she sat up and sat back. "What on earth are you doing here?" she asked Meghan. "I thought—"

"Half day of school today, remember? Teachers' meeting? Gosh, Mom, are you that old? Don't you remember anything?"

Libby refused to dignify the comment with a reply. Besides, she was too busy trying to figure out where the time had gone.

She glanced over her shoulder at the clock that hung on the classroom wall.

"It's nearly one-thirty!" Libby pushed back her chair and stood. She turned to Hal. "I'm so sorry I kept you this long. Your class was supposed to be over at noon. I didn't realize—"

"That's okay. I've got no place to go." He stayed right where he was, and when Meghan glared at him, he sat back in his chair and cocked his head, meeting her look with one that was easygoing and level. "Do you know how to knit, too?" he asked her. "Like your mom?"

"My mom is the worst knitter in the world. Even I could do better. Not that I'd want to. Knitting is boring."

"Actually, your mom is a pretty good knitter and a good teacher, too. You should give knitting a try. It's kind of cool."

"Yeah, whatever." Meghan shrugged. Her gaze flicked from Hal to Libby. "My dad doesn't knit."

If Hal realized there was an unspoken challenge in Meghan's words, he didn't acknowledge it. As calm as ever, he regarded Meghan as if she were some undiscovered species of animal and it was his job to figure out if she was dangerous. "He doesn't know what he's missing."

"My dad is an attorney. Attorneys are too important to knit."

"They are important." He turned in his seat just the slightest bit and just enough to let Libby know the next question was intended for her. "Does Dad ever help around the shop?"

Meghan, of course, missed the subtlety of the move. She rolled her eyes. "My dad lives in Pittsburgh. With his new wife."

"Ah!" Hal's gaze flickered to Libby. "Which explains the need for knitting therapy."

This was not the time to bare her soul. Not to a man who in spite of the easy friendship they'd established, was nothing more than a stranger. And certainly not in front of Meghan.

Meghan, who was—now that Libby thought about it— walking in too late to have just come from a half day of school.

Libby lambasted herself for losing track of the time. And her priorities.

Ever since Sister Mary Francis had told her that Meghan had arrived late for school—and Meghan had refused to say where she'd been and had insisted that the attendance taker in the office was wrong—Libby had come down on her daughter like a ton of bricks. From then on, when she dropped Meghan off, she sat in the car and watched her walk into the building. When she picked her up, she always got there right as the last bell rang so that Meghan saw her the moment she was out the doors. Today, thanks to the half day of school and Gwen's appointment with her financial planner, Libby had begrudgingly allowed Meghan to come home with Tanya, who was sixteen and already driving.

Now she saw the error of her ways.

"Where have you been?" She hadn't meant to make the question sound so accusatory, but it was hard not to. Before she trusted Meghan again, Meghan would have to earn that trust. "You told me you were coming right home."

"We did come right home."

"But not right after school."

Meghan's sigh could easily be classified as one of epic proportions. "I'm not in kindergarten."

The words *Then stop acting like it* were on the tip of Libby's tongue. She clamped her mouth shut and refused to go there. Fighting with Meghan in front of a customer was the height of rudeness. And besides, she knew it wouldn't get her anywhere. They'd gone at it plenty of times in the weeks since Libby had heard the bad news from Sister Mary Francis, and all their fighting had accomplished was to leave Meghan as gloomy as a storm cloud. That and tie Libby's stomach in knots.

She decided on a less confrontational approach. "Do you have homework tonight?"

"Do I have homework?" Meghan flounced toward the back of the shop. Even over the sounds of her stomping to the second floor and, from there, to the attic, Libby heard her loud and clear. "When do I ever not have homework? I wish I could just go live with Daddy and Belinda. At least they're married. It's way too gross to have to watch my own mother hanging all over some guy."

There were about a hundred different responses Libby thought of, not one of which managed to make its way past the knot of mortification in her throat.

She closed her eyes and drew in a breath designed to calm her. It didn't work. Neither did her fervent prayer that when she opened her eyes again Hal would have somehow magically disappeared.

He was still there, and she knew it was time to apologize.

"She's fourteen," she said, and because she knew that wouldn't mean anything to Hal unless he was the father of a fourteen-year-old, she tried a different tack. "If what I did might be construed in any way, shape or form as hanging all over you, I hope you'll forgive me. I didn't mean—"

He laughed.

It wasn't the response she was expecting and it brought Libby up short.

"You think that was funny?"

Shaking his head, he scraped his chair back and stood. "I think you're way too serious."

"Which you wouldn't say if you had any sense of what it's like to be a single parent raising a teenager. You don't have children, do you?"

"No." He gathered his knitting off the table. "And I think parenting is probably the toughest job in the world. But you've got me wrong. Parenting is definitely not what I think you're being too serious about."

"It's not."

He sidestepped his way around her and headed for the front of the store. Even though Libby tried to stay aloof, she found herself scrambling after him.

"Then what am I being too serious about?"

He already had his hand on the door and he stopped and turned to her. "Look," he said, "I don't want you to get the wrong idea and I don't want you to think I'm some kind of weirdo. But I'm a single guy. And my hand might be hurt and I might be going stir-crazy from being cooped up at home, but I'm far from dead. So the whole thing about you hanging all over me…" A smile tickled the corners of his mouth.

"Your daughter was overreacting," he continued. "She was imagining things. You were not out of line. You were not hanging all over me. But…" With a wink, he walked out the door. "It's a pretty interesting thought."

CHAPTER 9

Metropolitan Knits was closed on Sundays, so it was the perfect day for Libby to invite Gwen and Jesse over and cook dinner to thank them for all they'd done. In a rare show of enthusiasm, Meghan agreed it was a good idea. It was the right thing to do, she claimed, since Gwen was just about always in the store and Jesse had moved from fixing up the downstairs to working on the apartment and had started with the kitchen so that now they had a fan—and no more hole in the ceiling. Relieved to hear her talking so sensibly—or talking at all—Libby enlisted Meghan's help in getting out the china and silver, ironing the one linen cloth that fit the table in the dining room and putting the apartment in order.

That taken care of, she concentrated on the food.

Libby breezed through chopping the carrots, snow peas and red pepper and tossed them into the wok where the chicken was already cooking. She reached for a bunch of scallions, washed and waiting on the kitchen countertop. She liked to cook and she was good at it, too. It gave her a sense of satisfaction and accomplishment that she'd never found in knitting.

It also gave her something to think of other than Hal.

About to bring her knife down, Libby missed the stack of scallions altogether, and the blade smacked against the cutting board. She scolded herself as she had so many times in the days since Hal had come in for his first class.

If it wasn't for that smile of his, the way he winked at her and that throaty rumble in his voice when he'd said what he said about Libby hanging all over him—

"Mom! They're here!"

Meghan had been watching out the front window for their guests. She raced through the kitchen and down the stairs to let Gwen and Jesse in.

"And isn't it a good thing to get interrupted before my thoughts head somewhere they have no business going," Libby reminded herself. Her life was complicated enough, not to mention busy. She didn't have the time or the patience to deal with a man. She didn't want to deal with a man. She didn't need to.

Not even one as sexy as Hal.

"You're better off thinking about chicken stir fry." She turned to the kitchen door just as Meghan led Gwen and Jesse up the stairs and into the kitchen.

Apparently neither of them had listened when Libby had told them this was intended to be nothing more than a casual dinner, and suddenly in her jeans, gray crewneck sweater and sneakers, she felt underdressed. Gwen was wearing a vivid purple dress and, in deference to the cool September temperatures, a capelet knitted in shades of green from hunter to sage. Libby had seen her working on the garment just days before and was amazed that she'd already finished it. There was a little more gel than usual in Gwen's hair. The red spikes stuck up around her head like a crown.

Jesse, too, was transformed, and the difference was nothing short of amazing. He was wearing dark pants, a freshly pressed white dress shirt and a skinny black tie. He looked handsome and not at all uneasy about being dressed up. In fact, Jesse looked downright pleased with himself.

"So what do you think?" He had walked in carrying a paper shopping bag, which he set down on the floor, and held his arms out at his sides, showing off. "I clean up pretty good, don't I?"

"I'll say. You look like a country music star!"

"Oh, I don't know about that." He didn't smile. But then, Jesse never did. Libby was learning not to take it personally. He strolled into the living room and took the shopping bag with him.

"Dinner's almost ready," she called after him as she shooed Gwen out of the kitchen because Gwen, of course, wanted to help, and that wasn't the idea. "Meghan, honey, why don't you show Gwen and Jesse where to sit. I'll bring in the food."

"They know where to sit. They don't need me to tell them." Libby expected a roll of the eyes to go along with this statement, so she was surprised when Meghan grinned. "I'll help you instead," she said. "I'll put the salad in the bowls."

Libby wasn't about to argue, though had she been pressed, she might have questioned who this surprisingly cooperative young lady was, asked what had happened to the real Meghan and begged whatever aliens had abducted her and left a substitute in her place to keep her—just a little while longer.

Meghan's attitude went a long way toward adding to Libby's enjoyment of the evening, and she suspected that it put Gwen and Jesse at ease, too. During dinner their conversation was light and pleasant, and everyone made a fuss, first about the stir fry, then over the cheesecake Libby had made from a Palmer family recipe. By the time Meghan offered to pour coffee and brought the sugar bowl and a small pitcher of milk to the table, the sun was nearly down. The candles Libby had lit on the table added soft shadows to the room, and in keeping with the mood, everyone sat back, quietly satisfied.

Meghan got up and was back in a flash, a fresh glass of ice water in her hands and a look of anticipation on her face. "Well?" Jesse was sitting across from Libby, and Meghan went to stand at his shoulder. "Can we tell her now?"

"Tell me…?" Libby sat up, interested. Suddenly Meghan's new and improved personality was making more sense. She had something up her sleeve, though Libby couldn't imagine what. Not if it involved Jesse. "What are you two up to?" she asked.

"It's not something bad." Meghan jumped in with the

statement just so Libby didn't get the wrong idea right off the bat. "It's a good thing. A project."

"And whatever this project is, you've scammed Jesse into helping you with it."

"Now, Mom, it's not exactly like that." Jesse pushed back from the table. He stuck his long legs out in front of him and linked his hands behind his head. "It was actually my idea, so Her Majesty here—" he glanced over his shoulder at Meghan "—can't take all the credit."

Gwen was sitting on Libby's left, smiling like the Cheshire cat. It didn't take a genius to figure out that she was in on the secret, too.

"So everyone knows about this plan but me, right?" Libby waited for one of them to confess, and when no one did, she went right on. "You three must be pretty sure of yourselves. How do you know I'll say yes?"

"You've got to." Meghan dropped into the chair on Libby's right. "It's a great idea. A perfect idea. And it won't cost hardly anything, will it, Jesse?"

"Not hardly." The reflected candlelight in Jesse's eyes almost made it look as if he was smiling. "We've got a shoe-string budget and a brilliant plan."

"Which begs the question…" Libby looked around the table. "A plan for what?"

This was Meghan's big moment and the importance of the opportunity to state her case wasn't lost on her. She scooted forward in her chair. "The attic," she said. "Not a big room.

And nothing fancy. Just a bedroom and a walk-in closet and a sort of sitting room, you know, like a place where I could put my TV and my desk and do my homework."

Libby had been up to the attic only once and only when Meghan wasn't around. Meghan had staked a claim to the third floor space soon after they'd moved in, and Libby didn't want to violate her privacy. But what she'd seen had been less than impressive.

"There's only one big room up there," she said. "No walls to divide it and an open beamed ceiling. There's only one window over at the far end that overlooks the backyard and—"

"Jesse's going to put up walls." Meghan was as proud to announce this as if she herself had the skill to build walls. "He even said he could add another window. You know, as long as you don't mind if he cuts a hole in the side of the building. He can do it, Mom. Jesse knows how."

Jesse didn't confirm or deny this. He simply sat and waited for Libby's response.

"How much?" she asked.

Jesse had a piece of paper tucked into the breast pocket of his shirt. He got it out, unfolded it and looked it over. "We'll need drywall, spackle, paint, wire. All the usual stuff, plus heat ducts and some carpeting, too, but I know a guy who deals in remnants. Also, a good bit of insulation. We wouldn't want Her Majesty freezing to death in the winter or melting into a puddle of mush in the hot weather." He winked at Meghan. "Even so, I think I should be able to do it all for around six hundred. If…" He folded the list and tucked it back into his pocket. "If Meghan signs on as my assistant."

"I will!" Meghan could barely keep still. "I'll sweep up every evening when Jesse's done working. And I'll run errands. On weekends I'll help with the drywall and everything. And when it's all done, I'll keep my room clean. I swear I'll keep it clean! Please, Mom. Please! I can't share a room with my mother all my life. How gross is that?"

Libby thought of their current bedroom situation. She imagined a closet of her own and the luxury of a little privacy. All big advantages but not one of them as important as letting Meghan have a space to call her own.

She glanced toward Jesse. "Any chance of putting another bathroom up there?" she asked. Before Jesse had a chance to answer, Meghan threw herself in her mother's arms.

"I knew you'd say yes! I knew you would. I told you she would, didn't I?" Meghan asked both Jesse and Gwen. "And Gwen's going to crochet me an afghan to go in my new room, aren't you? Pink and purple. 'Cause two of the walls are going to be pink and two are going to be purple. Won't it be cool?"

"It will be very cool." Libby laughed. "Now somebody want to tell me how long this conspiracy has been going on?"

Gwen laughed. Jesse got up and went into the living room. He came back with the shopping bag he'd brought with him and held it in front of him, both his hands on the handle. "The attic," he said, "that's my special gift to Meghan. But I didn't want you to feel left out." He handed the bag to Libby. "So I brought one for you, too."

Libby peered inside the bag and saw something wrapped in tissue paper. She lifted the object, stripped off the tissue and found herself staring at the old, beat-up teddy bear.

He'd been cleaned and combed; his fur wasn't as matted. His sweater was washed. He looked at Libby with his one good eye.

As it had so many times before, a shiver of recognition raced through Libby. And just as she had so many times before, she refused to acknowledge it.

"I thought I told you to throw this away," she said to Jesse.

He took a sip of coffee. "You did. But I think that's because you don't remember Mr. Bear."

"You're right." Libby set the bear on the table. "I don't remember it. I've never seen it before. Not before I walked in here anyway."

"You sure?"

She wasn't, and the realization frightened her. It was exactly why she knew she had to pretend she didn't care. She turned to Gwen. "You know, I just was reading in a knitting magazine that there are people who knit sweaters for bears as a charity project. They give the bears to police departments and the police give them to abused children. I'll bet we can find a pattern for a sweater for a bear. Then this one can be displayed down in the shop."

"Just where your mother always kept him." The comment didn't come from Gwen but from Jesse. Libby had no choice except to turn his way again.

"You seem to know an awful lot about this teddy bear."

"Me and Mr. Bear…" Jesse scratched a finger over the bear's head. "We've been pals for a lot of years now." Over the bear's head, he looked at Libby. "Ever since the day you took Mr. Bear into that grocery store with you."

Libby didn't know how long she sat there stunned and silent. Her memory of the day Barb abandoned her was disjointed and foggy, but a little bit of it cleared, and she glimpsed the past. "I put him down," she said. "When I climbed the shelf to get the cookies. I left Mr. Bear on the floor."

Jesse nodded. "That's right where we found him when we went back."

Libby had been lost in memory. She shook it away and realized her heart was beating double time. The look she aimed across the table at Jesse was nothing short of accusatory. "*We? You* were the man with Barb in that grocery store?"

"My goodness, I had no idea it was so late!" Gwen hopped out of her chair. She hurried around to the other side of the table and wound one arm through Meghan's. "Come on, kid, let's get the dinner dishes cleaned up."

Meghan wasn't about to be left out. "But I want to hear the story," she said. "Come on, Mom!"

Libby didn't answer. She continued to stare at Jesse.

"Come on, guys!" Meghan implored anyone willing to listen. "This is all about Barb, isn't it? It's not fair if I don't get to hear it, too. She was my grandmother."

"And that means it's up to your mother to tell you the story. When and if she feels it's right." Gwen loaded Meghan down with dinner plates and silverware. "Let's go. March! If we finish fast, there's still time to catch some of the X-*Files* marathon on cable."

Libby never took her eyes off Jesse. She heard Gwen and Meghan leave. She heard the kitchen door close behind them. After that, she wasn't sure how long she and Jesse sat there in silence.

Finally he spoke. "Wasn't sure how you were going to take the news," he said.

She swallowed around the knot in her throat. "You could have told me sooner."

"What good would that have done?" He shrugged, not because he was uncomfortable, more because he knew it would have been futile to waste his breath on the story anytime before now. "You would have just tossed me out on my keister if I did."

"What makes you think I'm not going to do that now?"

Another shrug. He didn't look particularly concerned. "I never lied to you."

"You never told the truth."

"You weren't ready for it."

"And now you think I am?" Libby's voice was tight in her

throat. She clenched her jaw. "Do you think any time is the right time to tell me about the day you stole my mother?"

"Probably not." He had the good grace to admit it. Jesse stood. "But as long as we're getting the truth out in the open, you should know I stole her from you all right. But not that day. That day…" A shiver snaked over his shoulders. He twitched it away. "We were young and we were stupid and we were high," he said. "But I guess maybe you've figured that part out by now."

Her heart squeezed, but she refused to cry. She forced herself to look away from Jesse and caught sight of Mr. Bear. "How did you end up with him?"

Jesse poked his hands into the pockets of his pants. "Barb was never some raving lunatic drug addict. You know that, don't you?"

"Sure, that's why she abandoned her only child in a grocery store." The comment came out sarcastic. Libby meant it to.

"It wasn't like that." Jesse rocked back on his heels. "She didn't abandon you. She just forgot you. It was the pot. You know—" he held up two fingers in a V "—make love, not war."

"It's not something to joke about."

"I'm not joking." He slid into the seat Meghan had just vacated. "I'm trying to get you to understand. She was just a kid herself, twenty or so, and her husband—your dad—he was dead. Barb was depressed and she was miserable."

Libby jumped out of her chair. Hugging herself, she crossed the room to distance herself from Jesse and everything he said.

Jesse stood, too, but stayed right where he was. "We went back to the grocery store for you. A couple hours later. That's when we found Mr. Bear." He pulled in a deep breath and let it out slowly. "When she realized what she'd done, Barb just about went crazy. She went home, back to where the two of you lived with your grandparents, and by then they had you. They were spitting mad and who could blame them? They wouldn't let her anywhere near you. They told her they were going to see an attorney and they were going to get custody. Barb felt so guilty. She thought the only way to make things right was to beat herself up over the whole thing. That's why she ended up signing over her parental rights. She didn't think she was worthy to be your mother."

"So let me guess, after that she gave up you and she gave up drugs and she lived happily ever after. But that doesn't explain what you're doing here now or why she never tried to be a mother to me."

"You think?"

Libby held her breath. Did Jesse know everything about her relationship with Barb? And if he did, would he throw her part in the debacle in her face?

"You don't remember, do you?" he asked her. "The first day you went to school?"

Libby didn't even have to stop and think about it. Though

she had grown up loved and cared for by her grandparents, she had few memories of being a kid. None of them of the first day of school.

"I'm not surprised." Jesse nodded. "For a kid, starting school is a big deal, but in the great scheme of things it's not all that important. There's no real reason for you to remember. But, see, I remember your first day of school like it was yesterday. Because that day…" He walked into the living room and looked out the window, his back to Libby. "You see, *that's* the day I stole your mother from you."

"Come on, baby, it'll be groovy. You, me and the California sun. What do you say?"

Jesse Morrison was the most handsome man Barb Palmer had ever laid eyes on. And the sexiest. She hadn't seen him in nearly a year and time and distance had done nothing to diminish the impact he had on her. Just being near Jesse made her feel as if she were burning in hot lava. He was every fantasy she'd ever had and everything she'd ever wanted.

None of which changed the fact that the last time they'd talked she'd told him she never wanted to see him again.

Unfortunately that didn't stop her hormones from sky-rocketing when he leaned in close and whispered in her ear. "We can make love on the beach."

Barb was carrying an armload of newly spun wool. The small shop where she worked catered to a back-to-earth crowd of fiber artists and crafters who would go bonkers for this stuff.

She piled it on a table near the front door so they couldn't miss it when they walked in.

"No," she told Jesse.

He took a step back and stood up straight. "What do you mean no? Baby, it's me, lover-man Jesse. I haven't forgotten, baby. Not one minute of what we had together. It was good, wasn't it?" He drew out the Os in *good* so that the word fired her imagination. "I can't forget you. No matter what. I'm willing to bet you haven't forgotten, either."

He was right. Rather than cave—because caving would be easy, and easy wasn't something she deserved—she moved away and studied the new display of wool. She shifted a couple hanks of yarn from one side of the table to the other. "I said no, Jesse. I mean it."

"Yeah, but you're not serious." He peered at her face, but she refused to meet his eyes. She knew if she did she'd see nothing there but temptation. "The only thing Pittsburgh has going for it is smoke from the steel mills. Wouldn't you rather live somewhere with blue skies and sunshine? I've got this friend in San Francisco who says we can crash with him for a while." He gave her the little grin he knew always tickled her libido. "I've got the van packed and all set to go. We'll be in Indiana by this evening. Think about it—by tonight we could be lying together naked under the stars."

"No."

"Shit!" Jesse grumbled, not that he was angry, more like

he couldn't believe what he was hearing. "Are you telling me you really don't want to come?"

"I want—" She turned to Jesse but kept her arms wrapped around herself. It was that or risk running her fingers through his hair. "What I want is what I've been wanting all these months. I want Libby back."

Jesse backed off and backed away. "I thought you were over that."

Barb bit back a sob. "I screwed up. I should have fought harder to keep Libby. That's why I've got to try to make it up to her. If I stay here and work hard, if I show that I've changed—"

"You think those tight-ass Palmers are ever going to let you near her again?" Jesse shook his head. "Now that they've got her, they're never going to let your little girl go."

Barb's shoulders slumped under the weight of the knowledge. "Maybe that's not such a bad thing. The Palmers love Libby. They're taking real good care of her. Not like I did." Her memory of the events that led up to leaving Libby in the grocery store was hazy. The terror that had assaulted her when she'd realized what she'd done, though, was as clear as ever. The guilt, she knew, would never go away.

"So she's fine. And she's happy." Jesse pointed out the obvious. "What are you worried about? You can send her a postcard or something."

Barb sighed. "Even if I can't be with her, I want to be part of her life." That day her words were truer than ever. Barb looked at her watch. She'd have to get going and soon. "She starts school today. I always thought—" She swallowed the lump in her throat. "I always dreamed I'd be there to get her ready. You know, help her pick out what to wear and put her hair in a ponytail. I always thought—"

It was too much, and a tear slipped down Barb's cheek.

Jesse could sometimes be dense, but he wasn't insensitive. He came up behind her and wrapped his arms around her waist. "I get it. You love your little girl and you'd like to see her now and again. But you know, thinking about the way you'd like things to be isn't going to change anything. Neither is hanging around here wishing things could be different. That's why I want you to come with me. The guilt's dragging you down."

"Then maybe I deserve to be dragged down." She untangled herself from Jesse's embrace. "I'm going," she called into the back room where Margie, the woman who owned the shop, was working on the books. "I'll be back in a little while."

"Take your time!" Margie yelled back. "And give that little girl of yours a kiss for me."

Barb nudged Jesse aside. She was out the door in a minute and headed for Libby's school. If things worked out the way she'd planned, the Palmers would have dropped Libby off and left by the time she arrived. She'd have Libby all to herself. At least for a few minutes.

"You know if you don't come with me you'll regret it for the rest of your life."

She hadn't realized Jesse was in his van and slowly cruising down the street alongside where she was walking. Not until she looked over and saw that he had the passenger-side window down. "We're going to party hardy."

"I'm clean, Jesse," she said. "I have been ever since the day I ruined my daughter's life."

"Okay, so we won't party." Jesse had one hand on the steering wheel and he leaned toward the passenger door. "Would it make you happy if I said we wouldn't party?"

"It would make me think you were lying to me."

"Oh, baby, that's cruel!" When Barb turned a corner, Jesse turned, too, his pace matching hers. "You're going to break my heart."

She'd never wanted to hurt him, and though she'd never told him in so many words, pushing him out of her life had broken her heart. But if she'd learned nothing else in the past year, she'd learned there were some things in life more important than her own heart. One thing.

Libby.

They were close to the elementary school. Her heart in her throat, Barb stepped up her pace, looking over the sea of cars waiting in a line near the walk that led to the front doors.

Up ahead she saw Frank Palmer's blue Buick cruise to the curb and stop. She watched as the back door opened and Libby climbed out.

She was wearing a green-and-blue-plaid skirt and the blue

pullover Barb had knitted for her a couple years earlier. It had been big then, but now the sleeves ended just above Libby's wrists. Her little girl was growing up.

Libby had a pink book bag over one arm and she waved to her grandparents with the other.

The hardest thing Barb ever did was not race over to her.

Afraid to startle Libby, she took her time. Once she caught up, Libby was nearly at the steps that led to the front entrance.

"Hey, Libby Lou!" It was a silly nickname that Barb had always used. "How's Mama's little girl?"

Libby stopped and turned. She looked up.

"Mommy. It's you." Libby didn't seem surprised, just puzzled. But then she'd always been a serious child and never overly dramatic. She wrinkled her nose and chewed on her lower lip the way she used to do when she was finishing a picture in a coloring book. Barb's heart raced. "Grandma P said you were gone."

"I was gone. But I'm back now."

"Does that mean you're going to live with us again?"

The least she owed Libby was the truth. "The judge says you have to live with Grandma and Grandpa. But that doesn't mean we can't see each other. I wanted to see you today because it's your first day of school. That means it's special. I wanted to tell you to have fun. That I—" Barb's voice broke. She reached out a hand to pat Libby's dark hair. "I love you and I miss you."

Libby backed away from the touch. "Grandma P says you don't."

"She…she told you that?"

Libby shook her head. "She told Mrs. Miller. You know, the lady next door with the big hair and the smelly dog. I heard them talking. Grandma P told Mrs. Miller that you're a bad mommy. Are you?"

Barb stooped to be eye to eye with Libby. "Sometimes people make mistakes," she said. "Even mommies. I tried to be a good mommy."

"But good mommies don't leave their little girls in stores. I know because Grandma P told Mrs. Miller."

"She's right, of course." Barb forced a smile. It was brittle at the edges. It would have taken a stronger person than Barb to resist the pull of love she felt. She wrapped an arm around Libby's waist. "I love you, Libby Lou."

"No." Libby squirmed away. "You don't love me. You can't. Grandma P says so." From inside the building, a bell rang. "I can't be late," she said and she turned to head up the stairs.

Seeing Libby walk away, Barb panicked. She grabbed Libby, desperate for a hug and whatever comfort she could get from a kiss.

"I love you, Libby. I always have."

"No." Libby swatted at Barb. "You don't. You don't love me. Go away. You go away now!"

Barb didn't know what else to do. She loosened her hold, and Libby scrambled up the steps and ran inside.

It wasn't until the door closed behind her that Barb realized she couldn't catch her breath. She dropped to her knees on the sidewalk and clutched her stomach. Tears blinded her. She was deaf to everything but the sounds of her own sobs.

Until Jesse's arms went around her.

"Hey, baby." His voice was soft and he rubbed her back with one hand. "It's okay. She's just a kid. She didn't know what she was doing."

She was incapable of moving on her own, and he gently raised her to her feet. "I've got you," he told her. "And I'm not going to let you go. Not ever." Slowly they moved toward his van. "You just tell me what you want me to do. I'll do it, Barb. I'll do anything for you."

She looked over her shoulder toward the school and the door that had closed between her and her daughter.

She leaned into the protection of Jesse's arms.

"What you can do," she told him, "is take me away. I want to come with you, Jess. To California."

CHAPTER 10

In a voice mail that said something about a scheduling conflict and that he hoped she didn't mind, Hal canceled his second knitting class. Libby was glad. She had enough going on in her life without adding Hal into the mix.

Of course, she couldn't hide from him—or her potent reaction to him—forever. Though a doctor's appointment had forced him to change the time until later in the day, he showed up the next week as promised.

And with twelve inches of knitting on his needles.

"You're kidding me, right?" Libby looked at the knitting and groaned. It wasn't perfect, but it was way better—and far more—than anything she'd ever produced. "Fess up. You've got an old white-haired aunt stashed somewhere who's doing your knitting for you."

"Not a chance." He laughed and settled into a chair at the classroom table. He was wearing worn jeans—tight in all the right places, but Libby refused to acknowledge that she noticed—and a gray Ohio State sweatshirt along with sneakers that had seen better days. "I don't even know any little old ladies. I live in a loft apartment in a building that's chock-full of Generation Xers. There isn't even an old lady in my book discussion group."

"You belong to a book discussion group?" It struck her as out of character. Of course, that didn't excuse Libby from making it sound as if he'd confessed to cooking kittens. Or eating them alive.

Fortunately Hal didn't take her skepticism personally. He grinned. "I do know how to read," he said. "And I was bored after the accident. I live downtown, close to the main library, and they were discussing *The Da Vinci Code*. It's baloney." His grin got wider. "I had a great time starting arguments with the other people in the group. There's nothing like tossing a little Nietzsche or St. Augustine into the conversation to get people all fired up."

"You belong to a book discussion group and you're a philosopher?"

"Well, I do like to read. You know, on the days I go out on my boat on the lake. Not that I've been able to do that lately." He flexed his right hand, and Libby noticed that he seemed to move it with a little more ease than he had the last time she'd seen him. Still, it looked as if it hurt. "But, yeah, back when I went out on the water on a regular basis, I made good use of the peace and quiet."

"And so you read…?"

"Mostly philosophy along with biographies and a little bit

of Civil War history, but pretty much anything I can get my hands on. How about you?"

After listening to him, Libby felt positively unliterary, not to mention uncivilized. The only things she'd read in as long as she could remember were knitting magazines and the backs of cereal boxes, which she was too embarrassed to admit. "I don't have a lot of time to read," she said.

"How about to eat?"

It was one of those out-of-left-field questions, and she simply stared at him.

"You do eat, don't you?" he asked when she didn't answer. "You can't stay in the store twenty-four hours a day. You must get out once in a while."

"I do." She didn't, at least not much, but that was too pathetic to say. "Meghan and I were out just yesterday evening." Even as she thought about it, she cringed. She'd designed the girls' night out with the intention of hearing more about what was happening in Meghan's life. No such luck. Oh, Meghan had been as forthcoming as could be. She'd talked about Tanya and English class and how some girl in her homeroom had the coolest haircut and Meghan was thinking of getting one just like it, but she'd never once mentioned anything personal.

"I ate," she assured Hal. "Pepperoni pizza and a salad. So you see, I do get out sometimes. Occasionally. Once in a while."

"Good. Then you'll have dinner with me one of these nights?"

The question couldn't have surprised her more. Dinner? Surely Hal must have mistaken her for someone else. How could she possibly accept a dinner invitation from a man when she was Rick's wife?

Like a lightning bolt, the thought hit out of the blue, so ingrained and so automatic it took her a second or two to come to her senses.

"I can't," she said, even when she realized the only thing keeping her from accepting his invitation was her own insecurities. Her smile was fleeting. She sat down next to Hal and grabbed her own knitting from the table. "Thanks, but really, I…thanks."

"Okay." He didn't seem to take it personally.

But then Libby couldn't really be sure. She refused to meet his eyes.

"You ready to knit?"

The question should have come from her and the absurdity eased a bit of Libby's embarrassment. She managed a smile. "We can get started, but Gwen will be back in a couple minutes," she told him. "She said if you're ready, she'll teach you the purl stitch."

"What, you mean my favorite teacher doesn't want to?"

"Your favorite teacher…" Libby made a face. "I'm not ready for purling. I'm still having problems with the knit stitch."

Hal grabbed his knitting. "Come on." He encouraged her to take her work into her hands. "I think I figured out a couple tricks. Let me show you."

She wasn't sure. "If you show me, I'm going to have to refund your class fee."

"Or not." His answer was apparently final. He already had his knitting in his hands, and he waited for her to get ready to start. "Watch. See, if I hold my needles like this, kind of like chopsticks…"

She watched and repeated his movements. In no time at all she was knitting, and her stitches weren't nearly as tight as usual.

"Thank goodness!" Libby finished one row and started another. "Maybe by the time Gwen gets back I *will* be ready to learn to purl."

The bell over the front door that announced the arrival of customers rang.

"There she is now. Gwen!" Libby raised her voice and called out. "We're in the classroom. You want to teach us to purl?"

"I'm not Gwen." Meghan walked into the middle showroom. "I can't teach you how to purl, but I can show you this." She slid her backpack off her shoulder, unzipped it and reached inside. She pulled out a page of sketchbook paper on which someone had drawn a rose in watercolors.

"It's nice." Libby looked over the drawing. "Who gave it to you?"

"That's not the important thing." Careful not to bend it, Meghan put the drawing away. "The important thing is what I'm going to do with it." She raised her chin. "I'm getting it done. You know, as a tattoo."

"Over my dead body!"

Libby was already out of her chair, so in the great scheme of things it didn't matter that Hal put his hand over hers.

At least not to Libby.

Meghan, though, didn't miss a trick.

Her gaze slid from Hal to Libby. She narrowed her eyes. "You can't stop me," she said.

"Of course I can." It was so obvious as to be comical. Not that Libby felt like laughing. "I'm your mother. And you're underage. No reputable place would dare—"

"Come on, Mom, there are lots of places to get tattoos. They don't care if you have your parents' permission or not. That's how Tanya got hers."

"Tanya has a tattoo?" Libby didn't know where she was headed when she moved toward the door. Maybe over to Tanya's to ask her parents what on earth was wrong with them and how they'd raised a daughter who would even consider encouraging other kids to make the same mistake she did. Libby stopped directly in front of Meghan. "You're not doing it."

"Jesse has a tattoo."

"Jesse is an adult. You're not."

Meghan rolled her eyes.

"And don't give me that." Libby's insides roiled and she could barely put two coherent words together. Still, she somehow managed to keep her voice even. Not that she was worried that Hal would think she was some kind of Mommy

Dearest. She honestly didn't care. Not about Hal. Not at that moment. She didn't care about anything except Meghan.

She pulled in a breath. "Why don't you go on upstairs and get your homework done," she suggested. "We'll talk about it later. Like when you're twenty-one."

"I don't have to wait until I'm twenty-one. I can make up my own mind about things. Isn't that what you've always told me?"

Meghan was right, Libby had always encouraged her to think for herself. She'd just never thought the advice would come back to bite her. At least not this soon in Meghan's young life.

"When I said you could make up your mind about things, I didn't mean things like this. I meant—"

"Oh, come on, Mom, I'm not a baby!" If Meghan was trying to prove how mature she was, stomping her foot didn't help. "It's my body. I can decide what I want to do with it. You can't tell me."

"I can. I'm your mother and—"

The phone rang so Libby didn't have a chance to continue the argument. She excused herself from the classroom, told Meghan they'd talk later when they were both feeling more reasonable and went to get the phone behind the front counter.

"So you're actually there for a change?"

It was Rick, and for a moment the guilt she'd felt when Hal asked her to dinner came crashing over Libby again. She told herself to stop being ridiculous and thought about telling

Rick that she had a store full of people and she'd talk to him some other time. Reason prevailed. Except to talk to Meghan on her cell phone, Rick had never called since they'd moved to Cleveland. If he was calling now, it must be important.

"Hello, Rick." Libby kept her voice down and turned her back so she was facing the front window. There was no use letting Meghan know she was talking to her father. No doubt Meghan would use the opportunity to press her case about a tattoo. "How are you?"

"I'd answer that, but I think we have more important things to worry about than how I am. Besides, why would you care about me when you don't even care about Meghan?"

"Excuse me?" It wasn't much of a comeback, but it was all Libby could manage. "Did you say that I—"

"If you cared about her, you'd be there to look after her needs."

Libby's mind raced through the possibilities. She came up empty. Unless…

She didn't see how it was possible for Rick to know when she'd just found out, but she suddenly felt as if she had to defend herself. "If you're talking about the tattoo—"

"Tattoo? Meghan's getting a tattoo? Have you totally lost your mind? There's no way I'm going to let you allow my daughter—"

"She's *our* daughter." Libby shouldn't have had to remind him. "And, no, I'm not letting her get a tattoo. It was a joke, Rick." It wasn't, but he didn't have to know that. Even in a matter as small as this, it felt good to have the upper hand, and the inside track into what was going on in Meghan's life for once.

"Well, I'm not laughing. And it's no joke that I'm getting calls from Meghan's school either."

"The school called? You?"

"Yes, me. Why weren't you around to handle this?"

"I was…." Libby searched her mind. "When?" she asked. "Because if they called yesterday, I was helping a delivery driver unload an order. I thought I heard the phone ring, but I didn't have a chance to get to it in time and—" She listened to her own words and what sounded pitifully like an apology Rick had no right to expect. She gave herself a mental slap.

"I told you she's been having trouble adjusting in the note I wrote you, Rick, when I sent a copy of Meghan's test grades."

"I don't call three detentions 'trouble adjusting.' I call that major problems. If you can't handle her—"

"That's crazy." But it wasn't. More than once lately Libby had questioned her ability to give Meghan the kind of guidance she needed. She'd be damned, though, if she was going to admit it to Rick. "There's nothing going on here that I can't handle," she told him. "She's been grounded for not cooperating at school. And I've pulled her Internet privileges."

"I'm glad to hear it, because I'll tell you what, I can't spend my billable hours dealing with these things."

"Meghan is more important than your billable hours."

She heard him suck in a breath. "You're right. Of course."

She should have known what was coming next. It was the same strategy he'd used so many times over the years when he'd wanted to get his own way. It usually happened when Libby talked about doing something she really wanted to do, from going back to school to contacting Barb. His initial reaction was always anger. Then he throttled back to formulating a sensible argument. Next, she knew, he'd make it her problem.

"But, Lib…"

There was a time she would have responded to the subtle appeal in his voice.

"I don't have time for this stuff," Rick said. "You know that. I've got the firm to worry about. And Belinda's been put on bed rest. So you see, I've got a lot on my plate. And there you are, playing shopkeeper. I'm sorry to come down hard on you, but it's time for you to carry your part of the load, to be more responsible. Besides, it's your job."

She had just finished saying, "You bet it is, and I'm really good at it," when she realized he'd already hung up.

"Fine." She made a face at the phone. "Have it your way."

"Talking to yourself, honey?" Gwen breezed in and closed the front door behind her.

Libby didn't want to explain and knew if she was silent one moment too long, the older woman would see she was upset. "Hal's in the classroom," she said instead. "Wait until you see his knitting. He's ready to learn to purl."

"And I'm ready to teach him." Gwen was wearing a

handmade red ruana and she whisked it off and went on in. She glanced over her shoulder at Libby. "It's chilly out. Would you mind making me a cup of tea?"

She didn't. As a matter of fact, though she'd never before been a tea drinker, Libby had come to appreciate a cup once in a while, too. No more so than now when her nerves were frayed to the breaking point.

While Gwen greeted Hal and got down to business, Libby walked toward the kitchen. She almost didn't go inside when she realized Jesse was in there putting together a new bookcase.

They had spoken little since the Sunday Jesse came to dinner, and just thinking of the things they'd last said that night soured her stomach.

"You pretended to be my friend. How can you have the nerve to sit at my table and eat my food, then tell me something this horrible?"

"Doesn't take nerve," he's said. She pictured the way Jesse looked when he'd turned from the window. His gaze was level, his chin was high. "Just takes a man who's sorry for the part he played in the whole thing and thinks you deserve to know the truth."

"And that's supposed to make me feel better?"

"Nope. I wish it could. Then maybe I wouldn't feel so damned guilty about the whole thing."

"Guilty but not sorry."

He drew in a breath and let it out in a puff. "What do you want from me?" he asked. "I'm telling you the truth. It's about time somebody did."

Libby stepped back to give Jesse passage to the doorway, and at the time she'd thought the message was obvious. She waited for the message to sink in before she added, "I'll send your final check."

He didn't seem surprised. "And what about Her Majesty's bedroom?"

"I can find someone else to build a room in the attic. Someone who doesn't keep secrets."

"You mean someone who doesn't force you to take a look at your part in everything that happened."

Her first day of school might not have been what Jesse was referring to. For now, it was all Libby could bear to think about. "I was just a kid," she said.

"She loved you with her whole heart and soul."

For as long as she could remember, Libby had longed to hear those words. Odd how finally listening to them didn't fill her with the kind of warmth she'd always dreamed of.

Instead they left her empty.

With a shake of her head that brought her firmly back to the present, Libby shoved away the thought. Though she had yet to find the magic to do it, she suspected there might be a way to lock up the past and never think about it. It was a little harder, though, to ignore the present. Or that this was her store, and she'd be damned if she was going to cower in the corner.

She stepped into the kitchen. "I thought I fired you last week," she said.

"You did." Jesse kept right on tightening the screws that held the bookshelves in place. "I always was a slow learner."

"And you're still working on Meghan's bedroom."

"Can't disappoint Her Majesty." He finished with the final screw, stood the bookcase upright and stepped back to check his work. "So…" Jesse looked at her out of the corner of his eye. "I'm thinking you still haven't gotten over our little tiff the other night."

"Funny, it didn't feel little to me. It still doesn't."

"Then I'm sorry." He dipped his head. "Not sorry that I said anything, but sorry you took it the wrong way. All I ever wanted to do is help you understand. You couldn't. Not as long as you had your life in Pittsburgh. But now that you're here—"

Didn't he see that understanding was exactly what she couldn't afford to do? If she understood everything Barb had done, there was no way she could hang on to her anger. For years it was the only thing that kept her world glued together.

Rather than think about it or give Jesse a chance to get further into her head, Libby put on the kettle.

"Tea, huh?" Jesse didn't look at her when he asked. "Sounds to me like you could use something stronger."

"So now you're a mind reader?"

"I got ears," he said. "I know what's going on around here. Fighting with Meghan, a call from your ex. And Hal, of course."

"Hal is the only one who isn't bugging me." It was true, to a point. Hal wasn't bugging her the way Rick and Meghan were bugging her. At least not about the same things. Or in the same way.

"You're sure about that?"

There he went reading her mind again.

The cupboards above the sink were filled with sock yarn, and waiting for the kettle to boil, Libby organized it by color, the way it had been before an early-morning customer had messed it up. "I don't have time." It was all she was willing to say.

"For dinner? Or for a man in your life?"

"For either. The possibility..." A shiver snaked over Libby's shoulders and she shook it away.

Jesse didn't respond. He moved the bookshelf into place on the wall near the back door. She and Gwen had already decided that it was where they'd display yarns that were on sale, so that customers would have to see, admire and covet all the newer, higher-priced yarn before they found the discounted items.

"Mind if I tell you a story?"

The kettle whistled and Libby grabbed a pot holder and poured. "The last time you told me a story, I didn't like it."

"Chances are you won't like this one either."

"And you expect me to say yes?"

"I expect you to be open to possibilities. I thought that's what we were talking about."

"We're going to be late."

"We've got ten minutes."

"But if we're late…"

"Deep breaths, baby." Jesse was driving and he patted Barb's shoulder. It was early-morning rush hour, and though it wasn't anywhere near as congested as the traffic back in San Francisco, the Pittsburgh streets were crowded enough. He kept his eyes on the road. "It's going to be all right."

"Are you sure?" Barb tapped the passenger door of the van with her right hand to a rhythm faster than that of the Pink Floyd song playing on the radio. "I'm not so sure. What if Libby doesn't remember me?"

"How could a little girl forget her own mother?"

"But it's been so long." Barb dragged her purse into her lap. She fished out a compact and checked her face. She didn't wear much makeup; she didn't need to. She had a porcelain complexion and natural color in her cheeks. But Jesse knew that wasn't what she was checking. She'd been so excited about the prospect of seeing Libby again she'd spent most of their time back at the hotel pacing the floor. She hadn't slept a wink the night before. Her eyes were bloodshot, but there was nothing she could do about that. She snapped the compact closed and put it away.

"She's almost nine now."

Jesse knew this, but rather than say anything, he simply nodded.

"I'll bet she's tall."

"I'll bet she's a shrimp like you!" He laughed. "I'll bet she's got your temper, too. What do you think? Think she's hell on wheels?"

"Like I am?" Barb knew he was trying to get her mind off how nervous she was and she appreciated it. "You've never had it so good, Jesse Morrison."

She was kidding. He wasn't. He reached over and patted her hand. "You're right there! I don't deserve you, Barb." It wasn't the first time he'd told her that, but he knew he couldn't say it too often. "I'm a lucky man."

"You're only lucky as long as you stay clean." It wasn't the first time she'd told him this either, but Jesse didn't hold it against her. Knowing she was with him as he walked the road to recovery was the one thing that kept him going, step by step.

"I love you, Jess." She squeezed his hand. "I just want to make sure you're around for a long, long time. I don't want to be lonely anymore."

The light up ahead changed from green to red, giving him time to give her a peck on the cheek. "I swear, baby, my life is different now."

"And maybe mine will be, too. If the Palmers will let me visit Libby…" It was too overwhelming to even think about; Barb couldn't say any more. She held Jesse's hand tighter as they neared Riverview Park.

They turned into the entrance and cruised to a parking place near the swings. There was no one around. "It's not nine yet, is it? We haven't missed them?"

"We haven't missed them."

Jesse turned off the ignition, but he didn't move. "Go on," he said.

"Go?" Barb's voice bumped over the word. "You mean to wait for them? You're not coming with me?"

Jesse couldn't blame her for panicking. Ever since she'd gotten an unexpected reply to her last letter to the Palmers, Barb had been living with a full-blown case of the jitters. All she could think about was seeing her little girl again.

"Your in-laws don't exactly like me," Jesse reminded her. "I think this will go a whole lot better if I keep my nose out of it. I brought a book." He reached into the backseat and retrieved the copy of *The Big Book* that he'd gotten at his most recent AA meeting. "You visit with Libby and see how things go. If the coast is clear, well, then maybe I'll come over and say hello to the little lady."

Barb smoothed a hand over her sweater and fussed with her hair. "Do I look like a mom?"

"You are a mom."

She smiled her gratitude, then hopped out of the van.

According to what the Palmers had told Barb when they talked on the phone the night before, they'd meet near the swings. Jesse had purposely chosen a parking spot farthest from the play area. He angled his seat back and leaned back with it, the better to see but not be seen by the Palmers.

No use throwing gasoline on a fire.

There was no sign of the Palmers. Not at nine or even at ten. By eleven Jesse had had enough of watching the woman he loved poised on the brink of a breakdown.

Just as he jumped out of the van and headed over to where Barb was pacing, a car cruised by. He recognized Grandpa Palmer behind the wheel. Jesse ducked behind a tree.

Watching the Palmers park the car, Barb froze in place, her arms close to her sides, her hands curled into balls. Jesse didn't have to be close to know she didn't even take a breath. Her gaze was on the car, and when the door opened, she nearly jumped out of her skin.

Muriel Palmer got out. "I wondered if you'd still be here," she said.

The sound of the older woman's voice was like a slap. Barb craned her neck to try to get a better look at the car— and anyone else who might be in it. She closed in on Muriel. "Of course I waited," she said. "Is Libby—"

"Libby's fine." Muriel had a damp tissue in one hand and she opened and closed her fingers around it. "I wanted to make sure you really wanted to see her."

"Of course I do." Barb's eyes were bright with unshed tears. "I want to see her more than anything. I want to keep seeing her. I've been working and saving my money. I've got a job lined up, too. Right here in Pittsburg. It's with Margie at the yarn shop where I worked before we left for California."

"That's good." Muriel nodded. "Maybe you're finally growing up. Showing some responsibility."

Barb had always been responsible. Which is why she knew better than to argue the point. "I am," she said. "I know I wasn't a good mother to Libby…." She tried for another look into the car, but Grandma P was determined. She stood square in the line of Barb's vision.

Barb took a step to her left. "I screwed up," she said. "And I know I can't change any of it. But we could make a new start, if you'd let me. We could try to be a family again."

"It was never you. You know that, don't you?" Muriel held her hands together. She ripped the tissue in shreds. "It was the way you lived. The way you were acting. I know Jerry's death was hard on you, Barb. It was hard for all of us. But the drugs—"

"I'm clean. I have been for years. Ever since I realized what I did to Libby." As much as she tried, Barb couldn't help herself. She had waited too long for this moment. She took a step toward the car. "If I could see her—"

"She's not here."

The tension was all that had been holding Barb together. Hearing that she wasn't going to get to see Libby after all, it drained away, leaving nothing in its place but anger. Her cheeks flaming—just like her eyes—she glared at Grandma Palmer. "You said you'd bring her."

"I said you could see her. I didn't say today. We can't take any chances. You understand, don't you? We have to make sure you'll never hurt Libby again."

"But I have to see her." Barb's voice wasn't as angry as it was high and sharp, like the keening of a banshee. She grabbed Muriel's arm. "You said she'd be here."

It was all Frank Palmer needed to see. He flew out of the car, heading for where the women stood. Jesse had no choice but to race to Barb's side.

He didn't say a word. He didn't have to. One look at him and it was clear that the Palmers had already made up their minds.

They rushed back to the car.

"Wait! You can't go! You can't leave, not yet." Barb scrambled behind them. "You said I could see Libby."

Her hand already on the car door, Muriel turned. Her jaw was rigid. "I said I wanted to see if you had changed. If he's still around…" She glanced at Jesse. "You lied, Barb. Nothing is different."

"Everything is different. Don't you see?" A sob racked her, and she hugged her arms around herself and struggled for breath. "Jesse has changed, too. Besides, this isn't about him. It's about my little girl. You have to let me see Libby."

She was still sobbing when the Palmers drove away.

The tea was past ready.

Libby didn't pour it. Sometime while Jesse was telling his

story, her hands had curled into tight fists, and she slowly spread her fingers.

"I'm not sure I understand." Libby was a mother. She felt the pain of the Palmers' rejection, the desperation that must have filled Barb. She coughed away the tightness in her throat. "I thought we were talking about possibilities."

"We are." Jesse leaned against the new bookcase. "Think about it. What happened that day is what made Barb leave Pittsburgh for good. But the possibilities..." He pursed his lips, thinking.

She looked away. "You mean things could have been different."

"If the Palmers had opened themselves up to Barb, yeah. Who knows what would have happened." He pushed away from the bookcase and grabbed his toolbox. "They knew me as a loser. What they didn't know—or maybe they just didn't want to believe it—is that people can change. You never know what's under the surface. And you never know what can happen. But you've got to be willing to take a chance."

"Something tells me we're not talking about Meghan's tattoo." Libby managed a watery laugh.

"It's only dinner," Jesse said.

"Yeah, right." Libby set the teapot and cups on a tray. She had already hoisted all of it and started toward the classroom when she decided to add some shortbread cookies, too.

Maybe Jesse was right after all.

Maybe it was time for her to show Hal that she did, indeed, eat.

CHAPTER 11

"Where did you say you were going?" Jesse asked.

"I told you—dinner."

"Yeah, but that could be anywhere. Where did he say he was taking you?"

Libby had been doing a last-minute check of the outfit she'd decided to wear on her date with Hal—black pants, a white blouse and a black, red and white Fair Isle sweater Gwen had knitted for one of her daughters who, it turned out, had developed an allergy to wool. She turned away from the mirror on the back of the door of the restroom that the customers used.

"You're the one who said this was a good idea," she told Jesse.

"I did." He crossed his arms over his chest. "That doesn't mean I have to be happy about it."

Libby could have screamed. That would teach her for listening to Jesse's stories and making snap decisions based on emotions. "It's only dinner. Isn't that what you said?" She checked the mirror one more time, added some lipstick and decided enough was enough. She'd been obsessing about what to wear and how she'd look ever since earlier in the week when she told Hal she'd take him up on his invitation. "I thought you wanted me to be open to possibilities."

"Sure I do. But…" Jesse stroked his chin. "You think you know this guy well enough?"

Libby considered, but only for a moment. "No," she admitted. "I don't. But isn't that why you go out with somebody in the first place? To get to know them better?"

"Just not too well." Libby had left her purse in the kitchen showroom. She went to collect it and Jesse followed. "What time will you be home?"

This time she couldn't help herself and grumbled a curse. "You are not my mother," she reminded him.

"No, but if things had worked out differently, I could have been your father. Or at least your stepfather."

It was true, and though she'd never considered it before, Libby knew it meant she owed him. She watched him closely when she asked the question, "Why didn't you and Barb ever get married?"

Something told her that sooner or later he'd been expecting someone would ask.

His shrug wasn't much of an answer. "It was the sixties," he said. "We were all about free love. Or at least we said we were. Then the seventies came and women were hell-bent on proving they could have their own identities outside of marriage. After that, it didn't seem to matter anymore."

"But Barb left everything to you when she died."

She didn't mean it as an accusation, but Jesse didn't know

that. She might still be annoyed that he hadn't come clean about his relationship with Barb sooner, but it wasn't fair to give him the wrong idea. "I'm not begrudging you anything," she explained. "Barb left me the business and that's what's important. But she left you all her personal stuff, didn't she? That's why there wasn't anything in the apartment when we moved in."

"Wasn't sure how you would feel about walking into the place and finding Barb here and there. You know, clothes and books and things like that." He looked away. "She wore patchouli perfume, and I know what you would have thought when you found that. Dippy hippies! You would have tossed it right in the trash. Me? Every once in a while I spritz it in the air. Makes me think she's right there with me."

Libby's throat tightened. But before she could say anything, Jesse twitched his shoulders.

"I took her stuff to my place," he said. "Didn't know what kind of person you were or how you'd react to it all. If you want to look through any of it—"

"No. Thanks, really, but no." There was a time she might have jumped at the chance to get another peek into Barb's life. She wasn't so sure anymore. The things Jesse had told her had already skewed her vision of the world. "And, really…" There was a time that thanking Jesse for everything he'd done would have come naturally and sincerely. Now Libby found it hard to form the words. "I appreciate that you took the time to clean up the apartment. You and Barb didn't even live together, did you?"

"Didn't need to." He pursed his lips and she knew he was thinking back. "She had her shop and her customers and her knitting. I had my own handyman business. It gave us each a world of our own and interests separate from each other. It gave us some time apart, too, and you know, that's not such a bad thing in any relationship."

She thought of what it had been like working for Rick. They'd spent their days at the office together. They'd spent their nights talking about the days they'd spent at the office together. "I can see the advantages," she told him.

"Besides, your mother always said it was more romantic." It must have been a trick of the late-evening light, because Libby could have sworn Jesse blushed. "She'd invite me over for dinner a couple nights a week. I'd have her over to my place a couple others. Then we'd—" He cleared his throat. "Well, you don't need the details."

She didn't, but she was grateful for this glimpse into their lives. These days when they talked about the past, she was learning as much about Jesse as she was about her mother. "What ever happened to the 'free love' generation?" she asked him.

Before he could answer, the bell above the front door rang. Hal had arrived.

"Saved me from that discussion," Jesse said, and when Libby went to the front of the shop, he followed.

Gwen had beaten her to the door and she was chatting with Hal. Libby was used to seeing him in casual clothes, and for a moment she was at a disadvantage. Wearing khakis, a blue dress shirt and a tie, Hal looked better than ever.

She greeted him, then spun to face Jesse and Gwen, all her anxieties back in spades. "You guys and Meghan…you'll be all right together, won't you?"

"We've got a frozen pizza in the oven," Gwen said.

"Her Majesty is upstairs making a salad," Jesse added. "We'll eat, then we've got to get another coat on those walls up in the new room. After that, I'll head home."

Gwen grinned. "There's a Cary Grant movie on AMC tonight and I don't want to miss that! I'll watch until it's over. By then Meghan will be in bed. She says she's got plenty of homework to keep her busy this weekend and she's starting tonight."

"And the last of the invitations to the grand opening. Tell her not to forget those." Libby had left them on the kitchen table. The envelopes were addressed, but she'd asked Meghan to put the return address labels and stamps on them. "And remind her—"

"Yeah, yeah, yeah." Gwen put a hand on her shoulder and nudged her to the door.

Jesse held back. "By the time she's done with everything she has to do," he said, "you two will be practically home. Won't you?"

Hal assured him they would. He was still laughing when they got outside.

"Boy, those two are really something." Libby had never

paid attention to how Hal got to the knit shop. Now she saw that there was a silver Jaguar parked at the curb. He opened the passenger door and stood back so she could get in. "Doesn't it drive you crazy?" he asked.

"You mean all the fussing and all the attention?" When they pulled away from the curb, Libby glanced back at the store. Gwen was in the front room, watching out the window. Jesse stood next to her. "You know," she told Hal, "all the fussing and all the attention…it's really kind of nice."

Not long after they were on the road, Hal told her that he needed to pick up some paperwork at his shop. Then after, he said, they would have dinner on his boat.

"No way!" Okay, so it wasn't the most gracious thing to say to a man who was nice enough to cart her around in his Jag, but Libby felt justified. "I'm not dressed for boating," she pointed out. "And neither are you. Besides…" She watched as the scenery whizzed past the car. Even when they stopped at a red light, the trees kept moving. "Have you checked the breeze out there? This is no night for a landlubber to be out on Lake Erie."

Hal smiled, made small talk and didn't bring up the subject again. Libby breathed easier.

As it turned out, his shop was not all that far from hers. It was in a part of town called the Flats, the valley on either side of the Cuyahoga, the river that divides and defines the east and west side of Cleveland. The area is part commercial, part entertainment complex, and they cruised past the bars and restaurants just coming to life now that the sun was down. A few turns and the neon lights were nothing but memory. They were in the industrial part of the Flats, where the streets were narrower, darker and more deserted.

They stopped in front of a run-down warehouse with a sign above the door that badly needed paint. Libby squinted at it. The faded letters declared the place The O'Connor Brothers Boat Works.

"Brothers?" Libby got out of the car and followed Hal to the door, waiting while he unlocked it. "You didn't tell me you had brothers."

"I don't. My grandfather did. They were the ones who started this place. Their sons, including my father, inherited it. But my uncles...well, after working here as boys, they didn't want anything more to do with boats. My dad ending up owning the shop. Now he's retired in Florida and the business is all mine."

He opened the door and flicked on a light, then stepped back to let Libby inside first. She found herself in a reception area, and the reception area...well, it was not what she'd expected.

"What?" Hal closed and locked the door behind them. "You look like Alice just waking up in Wonderland. Not what you thought you'd find from looking at the outside of the building, huh?"

"I'll say." Libby glanced at the cherry paneling on the walls and the plush Oriental rug that was laid on a polished hardwood floor. There was a desk along the far wall, and to her right, leather chairs gathered around a low-slung coffee table. To her left, a brass plaque on a closed door read H. O'Connor.

"Aren't your customers intimidated?" she asked. "I mean, this isn't exactly what I think of when I think of boatbuilding."

"And not what anyone looking at the building from the outside would think of either." He gave her a wink and went over to his office. As he'd done before, he held the door for her.

Hal's office was even more spectacular than the reception area. More paneling. More plush Orientals. Art on the walls that was nautical and well done.

He noticed her amazement and smiled. "I love this location," he explained. "And it's ideal. Right on the river. Close to the lake. But, let's face it, no downtown is completely safe. I'd rather have the bad guys look at the outside of this building and think it's just another dump. So far, so good." He rapped his knuckles against the mahogany desk that took up a good portion of one part of the room. "Haven't had a break-in as long as I can remember."

There was a bookshelf on one wall, and while Hal went over to his desk to thumb through the paperwork there, Libby smiled her approval and looked over the titles. In addition to books on boat design, lake history and maritime legends, she saw books about St. Augustine and some by Nietzsche, too. "How many people work here?" she asked him.

"Including me? Seven. We're small but mighty." He found what he was looking for and slipped the papers into a leather briefcase that was on the floor next to the desk. "You ready to get on that boat?"

Libby winced. She was hoping he'd forgotten.

"It's a lovely thought. Really." A lovely thought that chilled her to the bone. She rubbed her hands over the sleeves of her sweater. When Hal walked to the far end of the room where there was another door, she followed, convinced that if he'd just listen, he'd see the reason in her argument. "I didn't even bring a jacket.. And my shoes..." She pointed to her black leather pumps. "No way these are appropriate. I just didn't think—"

"Come on." He put a hand to the small of her back. "Stop worrying. I'm not going to let you freeze to death."

He opened the door, turned on a light switch, and Libby stepped into the warehouse. Here, the floor was utilitarian concrete and the ceiling soared thirty or more feet over their heads. The building was massive, with windows high up on three of its walls. The fourth wall, which faced the river, was made entirely of glass.

She was moving that way even before she knew it, pulled by the beauty of the rippling water and the last rays of violet light that illuminated the sky. To her left and a few hundred feet to the north, the river emptied into Lake Erie, and she saw whitecaps churning the open water. Between the warehouse and the lake was an old steel railroad bridge, its beams looking like lacework against the slightly brighter sky. Across the river was a restaurant, and although it was too chilly for anyone in their right mind to be out on the patio, thousands of tiny white lights twinkled around the deck and in the branches of trees that swayed in massive planters. The lights were reflected in the river like a million stars.

She turned from the scene, all smiles.

"You like?" Hal was smiling, too. He wasn't looking at the scene, though, he was looking at Libby.

"It's wonderful. And during the day the light must be perfect. What a great place to knit!"

"Oh, no." He laughed. "Knitting is my therapy, remember. It's not my vocation like it is yours. It's not even my avocation. There's definitely no knitting going on here. The guys would ride me forever if they saw me with those needles in my hands. Nope, nothing happening here but boatbuilding. Come on, I want you to see the ladies."

What he hadn't bothered to mention was that the ladies in question weren't just boats. They were luxury yachts, and seeing them took Libby's breath away.

He grinned at her awestruck expression. "So what do you think?"

Libby skimmed her hand against the wooden hull of the nearest boat. "When you said boats, I was thinking little putt-putt motorboats. You know, the kind people fish from."

"People fish from these." He rested one palm against the boat. "These people fish the Mediterranean. And the folks who ordered that one—" he looked across the wide aisle to where another yacht waited. "—they're planning on sailing the Caribbean and I wouldn't doubt if they tried a little fishing while they were there. If we ever get the boat finished."

"You will. Soon. You're making great progress."

He didn't look convinced. "I'm making progress, I don't know how great it is. Fortunately the guys who work for me are terrific. They're really picking up the slack." He flexed his right hand and gritted his teeth. "One of these days I'll be back at it with them instead of just standing around watching."

"Something tells me you do a whole lot more than just stand around and watch. Let me guess—you meet with the customers, draw up the plans, do the schmoozing."

He still had one hand against the boat hull to Libby's left. He put his other hand to her right. His aftershave wasn't one she recognized; nothing Rick ever wore. It was musky and masculine and, as its designer had no doubt intended, the scent went right to her head.

"You think I'm good at schmoozing?" The overhead lights added a glint of mischief to his eyes. Hal leaned toward her, his lips a hairbreadth from her. "You ain't seen nothing yet!"

"I can imagine."

"And…?"

She wasn't sure what he was getting at. Or maybe she was and she just didn't want to admit it. "And what?"

"And do you like what you imagine?"

This was too much. Even for a woman who was trying her darnedest to act sophisticated. Her cheeks on fire, Libby ducked under Hal's arm and backed away, making sure she smiled while she did it. She didn't want to send the wrong signals and make him think she wasn't interested. It was just that—

"I'm moving too fast."

"You're reading my mind."

He scratched a hand over his chin. "It's been a long time since I met a woman as attractive as you."

"I'm flattered. Really. But it's been a long time since…" She realized what she was saying and laughed. "It's been a really long time since I did any flirting. Or any dating, for that matter. You're going to have to cut me some slack, I'm a little out of practice."

"Fair enough." As if she'd just told him to stick 'em up, he held up both hands. "I promise not to come on so strong. And you…what are you going to promise?"

She would have liked to tell him she promised to be the woman of his dreams, but that was going a little too far. She was having a tough enough time living up to her own. "I promise to try," she said. "Try what, I'm not sure, but I promise to try. Try to be a little more relaxed, maybe. Try to enjoy the moment without worrying about invoices and inventory and all the things I usually worry about. Maybe I need to follow Jesse's advice and be a little more open to possibilities."

"It's all I can ask." He offered her his arm. "Now how about the possibility of dinner on my boat?"

"Hal, really." Even though she took his arm, she locked her knees and refused to move. "I can't."

"You said you'd try."

"I didn't say I was going to try anything foolish. Anyway, I thought you had to wait for your hand to get better. You know, before you can take your boat out again."

He gave her a tug. "Who said anything about taking the boat out?"

He stopped in front of the next boat, bowed at the waist and waved her toward the scaffolding that had been put up next to it to provide easy access to all its levels. "Ma'am," he said, "here she is. The *Moira O'Connor*, named after my grandmother, by the way, and she can be just as temperamental as Granny when she has the mind. Like I said—" he looked up toward the deck "—dinner is served on board."

She gave him a playful whack on the arm. It seemed the only fitting response after the way he'd strung her along. With Hal's hand on her arm to steady her, Libby climbed up the scaffolding and stepped onto the deck. He was at her side in a second.

"Welcome aboard," he said. Totally at home and as proud

of the boat as any man could be, he moved toward a table and chairs that had been set up near the back. Stern or aft, she wasn't sure what the correct term was and she wasn't about to ask.

Libby took a deep breath. "Something smells wonderful." There was a Crock-Pot plugged in near the table. "Don't tell me you cook, too."

"Only if you count burgers on the grill and the occasional fish I catch myself." There was an ice bucket nearby, and he got a bottle of wine out of it and uncorked it. He poured and handed Libby a glass. "The good news is Darlene, my receptionist, is a great cook. But then, she's got something like seven kids, so she's had plenty of practice. She's a good sport, too. She threw together dinner and she assures me it will be done to perfection by the time we're ready to sit down and eat. Until then..."

He toasted her with his wineglass and took a drink, then grabbed her hand and headed toward the front of the boat. "She was built in 1922," he said. "Just about the same year as Granny, but don't tell her I told you so. She's really touchy about her age. She's seventy-seven feet long and has a deck of fifty-four feet. What you're walking on is Douglas fir, but the hull is constructed from mahogany over cypress. She weighs forty-one tons—considerably more than Granny— and she can do ten knots. I'm in the process of refinishing and refurbishing her stem to stern. If you're willing, tolerant enough to listen to me carry on and not afraid of being bored to death, I'd love to show you around."

* * *

As it turned out, Hal did not bore her to death. Though she knew nothing about boats and even less about restoring one, Libby was fascinated. And impressed. From the state-rooms belowdeck to the wheelhouse, the *Moira O'Connor* was gorgeous. Hal was proud of the boat. He had every right to be.

Another thing he'd been right about was Darlene. She was, it seemed, something of a wizard when it came to Crock-Pot cooking. She'd combined chicken with vegetables, added rice and Cajun seasonings and produced a dish so mouthwatering Libby had seconds. She could only hope the woman was half as talented when it came to being a receptionist. If she was, Hal was in good hands.

"Fabulous. All of it." Libby sat back, content. When they'd sat down to eat, Hal had lit candles in the center of the table. The flames danced in a draft and the light threw soft shadows against the walls. "The chicken and the salad and the bread."

"Darlene gets no credit for the bread," Hal said. "I picked that up myself at the grocery store."

"And you did a good job of it!" Libby laughed. In the short time they'd spent together she'd learned a few valuable things about Hal. Number one, he loved his boat, and honestly she couldn't blame him. Number two...

She sipped her wine and studied Hal. The second thing she'd learned was even more important—she liked Hal. He was funny and easy to talk to. He was smart enough to discuss politics, the economy and—every once in a while and only when he knew he could get away with it and not come off looking too erudite—philosophy. He had a silly side, too, and little could he know how much she appreciated the chance just to let her hair down and relax. What with everything that was going on at the shop and Meghan—

Libby sat up, suddenly aware that she'd been having so much fun she'd lost track of the time.

"Dang! I told Meghan I'd call at eight." She hadn't worn a watch. "How late is it?"

He checked his watch. "It's a bit after nine-thirty."

"You don't mind, do you?" she asked, but before he had a chance to answer, she already had her cell phone out and was making the call.

"Meggie, hi!" Though she told herself it was crazy, Libby breathed a sigh of relief when Meghan answered. It was an illogical response, but if Libby had learned anything lately it was that when it came to parenting, logic was overrated. Of course, Meghan was staying put that night, but there was nothing like the sound of her voice to reassure Libby. "Is Jesse gone?"

Meghan told her he was.

"And Gwen?"

"Still watching her dumb movie."

"And you're doing what? Homework?"

"Some."

"My invitations?"

"They're done. How long you gonna be gone?"

It wasn't until she was tempted to say *forever* that Libby realized how much stress she'd been under. And how nice it was to take a break. "We're just finishing up dinner."

"All right." Libby could have sworn Meghan wasn't even listening. "See you later. 'Bye." She hung up before Libby could say another word.

"Well, I guess that'll teach me to be caring and concerned." Libby flipped the phone shut.

Hal didn't seem surprised. "Something tells me there are better things to do on a Friday night than talk to your mom on the phone."

"Not for Meghan, there aren't." Libby tucked her phone into her purse. "She's not going out and she's not to have anyone in. She knows the rules."

"Uh-huh." The way Hal said this made it sound as if Libby was just about the dumbest person in the world.

She wasn't and she knew it. So did he. Which didn't mean she didn't feel the need to defend herself. She set down her wineglass. "Oh, come on. Meghan can be difficult. I'll admit that. She can be headstrong. But she's not going to hog-tie Gwen and go out."

It was obvious Hal wasn't willing to argue the point. But that didn't keep him from saying, "I would have. Not hog-tied Gwen, of course, but when I was that age, back in the good old days before parents with cell phones could check up on kids anytime, I'd wait until my parents walked out the front door, then—whoosh—I was out the back! Most of the time they never even knew I was gone."

"Boys are different." Libby was sure of this. That didn't explain the sudden uneasy feeling that tightened her stomach, though. "You don't think—"

"I shouldn't have said anything. I'm sorry." He'd already told her not to worry about the dishes and he cleared them away and loaded them into a tub. There was an employee break room on the other side of the building, he'd told her, and they'd clean up later.

"Look…" He sat down across from her and reached for her hand. "If it will make you feel any better, call back. You can always say you forgot to tell her something. Meghan will answer the phone. Or Gwen will. Then you'll feel better."

"I'll feel like I'm insecure and have an overactive imagination."

"So you're insecure and have an overactive imagination. Something tells me that's part of what good parenting is all about. Hey, I'm looking out for myself here." He bent his head and looked her in the eye. "I was just going to suggest we grab the rest of the wine and watch the river roll by. Can't have you worried about Meghan when I'd rather have you thinking about me."

Libby was torn, but there never really was a question about what she'd do. She fished her phone out of her purse and called home.

There was no answer.

"Gwen must have dozed off in front of the movie," Libby said.

She tried Meghan's cell phone.

There was no answer there either.

"Well?" Hal sat back. "You're in charge here. You tell me what we should do. The closest I come to parenting is being an uncle to my sister's kids, and they live in Colorado and I only see them once a year. I'm the guy who takes them to baseball games and feeds them too much junk food. Something tells me those skills aren't going to help in a situation like this."

They wouldn't. But neither would panicking. Easy to say and not so easy to do.

Libby tried both numbers again.

Still no answer. *Disappointment* was too mild a word.

"I'm sorry," she said. She gathered up her purse and stood.

"I'm not." He blew out the candles. "Oh, I'm sorry you have to go through this. I'm sorry kids aren't more responsible. I'm sorry we're not going to get to sit and watch the lights on the river and hope an oar boat passes by, too. But, hey, we'll find another night to do that. What I'm not sorry about is helping you out." He offered her his hand. "Come on, let's get you back home and see what's up."

They were back at Metropolitan Knits in just a few minutes, but even before Libby climbed the stairs to the apartment and, from there, checked out the new room in the attic, she knew nobody was around.

She called Jesse, who assured her Meghan had been upstairs where she belonged when he'd left. Libby called Gwen, too, but there was no answer at her place. She tried Tanya, too, who swore she knew nothing about Meghan's whereabouts.

Finished with the last of the calls, Libby drummed her fingers against the front counter. "It's getting late," she told Hal. "You should probably just head home."

"I'd rather stay." It was clear he wasn't sure how she'd react to the offer.

"You don't need to."

"And you don't need to carry all the responsibility yourself." He grabbed her hand. "What do you think? Will she be more surprised when she walks in and finds us down here? Or upstairs?"

Upstairs was home and far too personal. Libby felt bad enough about inconveniencing Hal by making him wait with her at the store.

They sat in the classroom. Hal looked interested in what was going on but not all that worried. He linked his fingers behind his head, tipped his chair back and waited. Libby tried Meghan's cell phone again. Rather than pacing and betraying the fact that she was nervous, she grabbed the shawl she had started knitting with Gwen a few weeks earlier.

These days, the knit stitches were getting easier. And the yarn overs that added a long drapey stitch to the pattern weren't bad either. But when Libby tried to knit two stitches together...

She poked her needle through the second stitch from the end of the needle, pushed too hard and ended up knocking both stitches off.

Fortunately she didn't have to struggle—or worry—for long. Meghan knew better than to use the front door. She came in the back way, and from the sound, Libby knew she already had one foot on the steps that led up to the apartment when she called out.

"Meghan, we're in here."

Meghan's eyes were wide with horror when she walked into the classroom. Her face was ashen. "You said you'd be out a while longer."

Libby set down her knitting. "I would have been if I'd known what was going on. Where's Gwen?"

"Her grandson, Eli—you know, the kid with the cool car? —he was in an accident. He's okay, but Gwen went to the hospital to see him and—"

"And you told her not to worry, you'd call and let me know she was gone."

Meghan swallowed hard. "It's no big deal," she said. "I just went—"

"It's a very big deal." Libby voice shook with anger. "You lied to me."

"I just went out. To Tanya's."

She stared at Meghan. "You're sure?"

"Yeah." Meghan was wearing her new jeans, a T-shirt with Scooby Doo on the front of it and a black jacket. She shifted her shoulders and refused to meet Libby's eyes. "I'm home now, right? So what difference does it make? You two—" she slipped Hal a look "—you're acting like I robbed a bank or something."

"But you didn't, did you, Meghan?" As casually as if they were talking about the weather, Hal got up. He crossed the classroom. "Not that it's any of my business, but..." He glanced at Libby. "You don't mind?"

She didn't, though she couldn't guess what he was up to.

"I think we can get this whole thing out in the open right now, don't you?" He brought a hand down on Meghan's shoulder. It was nothing more than a friendly pat, but she winced and tears sprang to her eyes.

Libby was no fool. She knew exactly where Meghan had been. "You didn't." Her knees shook when she stood. "Meghan, you went and got a tattoo, didn't you?"

Meghan shot Hal a look. She sniffed and stripped off her jacket. She tugged down the neckline of her T-shirt. There was a tiny red rose on her shoulder blade, and sure that they'd had a good look at it, she spun, grabbed her jacket and headed upstairs. "You bet I did," she called to them. "And now that I have it, there's not a thing either one of you can do about it."

CHAPTER 12

"I've made up my mind. I'm never going to date again."

Though it really had taken her no time at all to make her decision, to Libby this was a weighty announcement. She would have appreciated it if Gwen didn't greet it with a cackle of laughter.

"What?" It was the morning after her date with Hal and they were unpacking an order of alpaca yarn that Libby had bought for a song from a local breeder and spinner. She could mark it up minimally and still make money, and it would make a great featured special at the grand opening. Her arms were filled with hanks of yarn when she shot a look at Gwen. "You want to tell me why that's so funny?"

"It's more than funny. It's ridiculous." Gwen grinned when she said this, which was why Libby didn't take her response personally. "Lighten up, honey." Gwen piled the yarn into a big wicker basket. She held out her hands and Libby tossed more yarn her way. "You're overreacting."

"Oh, no. I don't think so." It was a good thing alpaca was so wonderfully soft; when Libby clenched her fists, her hands were cushioned by the yarn. "There is no such thing as over-reacting. Not to a tattoo." Just thinking about it made her shake her head in anger and dismay. "Meghan has mutilated herself. Permanently."

Libby relived that first shocking moment of seeing the rose, the size of a quarter, on Meghan's shoulder blade. Now, as then, it made her feel queasy. "The whole idea is hideous. I mean, letting someone get that close to you with a pen or a knife or whatever it is they use to inject the ink into your skin…" A new thought hit and she shuddered. "You don't suppose they made her take her shirt off, do you? In front of people?"

Gwen walked away from the yarn basket, scooped the alpaca out of Libby's arms and led her over to the classroom table. Both hands on Libby's shoulders, Gwen pressed her down into one of the chairs.

"My guess is she wore a tank top under her T-shirt," Gwen said, and Libby didn't know if this was true, she only knew it made her feel better. "And, believe it or not, I'm not insensitive to how you feel. This is major." Of course Gwen would understand. She was, after all, a mother herself.

"It is." When it felt as if she might start crying again—the way she'd cried most of the night after Meghan had gone to bed and Hal had left—she worked over her bottom lip with her teeth. "I've tried so hard," she told Gwen. "All Meghan's life, I've tried to be a good mother. Then this happens. Can you imagine what Rick is going to say?"

"What Rick is going to say, Rick is going to have to say to Meghan. She's the one who did this to herself."

"But I'm the one who let it happen. If I hadn't gone out last night—"

"There you go again, blaming yourself. Listen, if there's one thing I learned during all those years my kids were growing up it's that you can't do their thinking for them. Oh, you can try. But the more you try, the more it doesn't work. Eventually you learn that you've got to let them make their own mistakes."

"But she's only fourteen!"

"Yeah, there's an interesting thought! Chances are, there are worse things than tattoos in your future!"

Gwen was trying to be funny. She was trying to make Libby feel better.

Neither worked. Especially since Libby knew Gwen was right.

Libby's shoulders sagged under the weight of her guilt. "That's exactly why I'm swearing off dating. Once and for all, forever and ever. If I never leave her alone—"

"She'll grow up having weird issues and she'll blame her psychological problems on you."

"Better to have weird issues than tattoos."

"You think?"

"I don't know!" Libby threw up her hands in frustration. She wasn't in the mood for philosophical questions. She'd heard enough of that from Hal the night before. Oh, he'd tried to be understanding and supportive, but it was clear from the start that a man without children couldn't possibly comprehend the enormity of the situation.

No doubt, through it all he'd learned a thing or two about Libby. Like that she might be a levelheaded businesswoman who was organized and on the ball regarding Metropolitan Knits, but when it came to her daughter, reason and logic went right out the window.

Imagining the scene only made her feel worse, and Libby decided that maybe it wasn't such a big deal to swear off dating. After the way she'd ranted and raved and carried on about Meghan's tattoo and Meghan's irresponsibility and Meghan's disregard for her own health and safety, Libby was pretty sure she was never going to see Hal again anyway.

She groaned and dropped her head into her hands. "I can't believe I failed this miserably. I was the world's worst date. And I'm the world's worst mother."

Gwen patted her shoulder. "Oh, honey! You've got this all wrong. Just because Meghan got a tattoo doesn't mean you're a bad mother. All it means is that Meghan's a teenager. She's going to make mistakes."

"But I don't want her to. I want her to have a good life."

"And she will." The bell over the front door rang and Gwen headed that way. "You'll see," she called over her shoulder. "Right now it feels like the end of the world, but she'll come through this and—oh!" Gwen came scrambling back to the classroom. "Something tells me this is for you."

Unless it was a one-way ticket to a tropical island where no one knew her name and nobody could find her, Libby was pretty sure she wasn't interested.

Her sense of duty overcame her fantasies. If there was a customer who needed her help or an order that needed her signature…

She dragged herself out of the classroom and went to the front room. There was a delivery man standing just inside the door. He was holding a vase of the biggest, most gorgeous roses Libby had ever seen. They were pink. Vivid and brilliantly pink.

"Libby Cartwright?" The delivery man thrust the flowers into her hands and turned for the door. "There's a card," he said, "attached to the bow. Have a nice day."

The vase was enormous. Rather than risk dropping it, Libby clambered to the front counter and set it down. She traced a hand over one of the fragrant pink petals. "It's got to be from Grandma and Grandpa P. They've got their dates mixed up, the poor darlings. They must think the grand opening is tomorrow, not next week. There's no other reason anyone would send me—"

"You could open the card and find out." Gwen leaned over her shoulder.

"Of course!" There was absolutely no reason for her to be nervous, yet Libby's hands shook when she unpinned the envelope from the white gossamer ribbon tied around the vase. There wasn't an inscription on the card that read *Con-*

gratulations or *Good luck*, just a note written in unfamiliar handwriting.

Libby read the message out loud. "We still need to sit and watch the river." Her surprise couldn't have been more complete. A thread of anticipation curled through her, and rather than stammer and betray her feelings, she cleared her throat and started again. "We still need to sit and watch the river. The night before the grand-opening party?" She looked from the card to Gwen. "It isn't signed."

Gwen smiled broadly and moved the vase of roses to a place of honor next to the cash register. "It doesn't need to be; does it? The boy's got good taste."

"He's just being polite." It was a distinct possibility.

"Uh-huh." Gwen messed with the ribbon. "Lots of guys spend a hundred bucks on flowers just to be polite."

"He knew I was upset." That much was true. The way she'd carried on, Hal would have had to be comatose not to notice. "He's just trying to make me feel better."

"He could have done that with an e-card."

"He probably isn't used to dating women with children. I caused a scene. He was uncomfortable. He's embarrassed and doesn't know how to handle it and flowers are the perfect way to do that. They're personal but not too personal."

"Flowers and another date?" Gwen stared at Libby, and Libby knew she'd go right on staring until Libby admitted the truth.

A smile dissolved her solemn expression. "He likes me," she said.

"He sure does, honey!" Gwen giggled like a kid. "You're going to take him up on his offer, aren't you?"

There was nothing like disappointment to dissolve anticipation. Libby's smile faded. "I'd like to, but—"

Gwen would have none of it. She rounded the counter and took the card Hal had written out of Libby's hands. "Do I have to read it to you again? Just so the words sink in?"

"No, but—"

"He's got awfully good taste. If he's this good with flowers, imagine what he's like when it comes to jewelry."

"You're jumping the gun here, don't you think?"

"Am I?" There was devilment in Gwen's eyes. "Ever think that a man's enthusiasm for sending flowers might say something about his enthusiasm for other things?" She gave Libby a broad wink and a playful elbow in the ribs. "You know what I'm talking about, girlfriend."

Libby did and it was way too early in her relationship with Hal to even consider. Then again, she couldn't remember the last time Rick had sent her flowers.

With a shake of her head, Libby got rid of the thought.

"I told you, Gwen, no more dating. As much as I'd like to—"

"You would like to, wouldn't you?"

There was that look again, grandmotherly and as probing as a laser. Libby turned her back on Gwen. It was a little harder to turn away from the truth. "Yes," she said. "I'd like to. But I'd also like to see my daughter graduate from high school. To watch her move into her dorm at college. To be at her wedding and see my grandchildren grow up. I want Meghan to be well-adjusted and happy. I never want her to get into trouble or do the wrong thing. I've got to think of her first."

"And you think teaching Meghan that a mother has to sacrifice every aspect of her life for her children, that she has to lock herself away and not have any fun and never have a relationship she finds fulfilling…you think that will help her grow up to be well-adjusted, how?"

"All right." Libby surrendered with a sigh. She wondered if it fooled Gwen. As much as she tried to pretend she was agreeing to a second date with Hal out of some sort of deep-seated need to show Meghan the advantages of having a well-rounded life, she knew the truth was far simpler than that.

She wanted to go. She wanted to see Hal again.

Just thinking about it set off a sizzle of anticipation.

Until the cold hand of guilt came by and froze it with a touch.

"One more time, but that's it," she vowed and she got back to unpacking the alpaca yarn. "After that, I swear, I'm never dating again."

She couldn't wait to do this again.

Libby watched the downtown scenery glide by outside the Jag. She leaned back against the leather headrest and sighed.

Anticipation wasn't all it was cracked up to be; her date with Hal was nicer than she'd even imagined.

"You're looking mighty happy with yourself." From the driver's seat, Hal reached over and gave her hand a squeeze. "What are you thinking?"

"That things are turning out all right." Nobody could have been more surprised than Libby to admit it. Then again, the Libby who'd uprooted her life and established herself in a new city just a few months earlier was a woman she hardly remembered. "We're all set for the grand opening tomorrow. I've got it all together," she said, then laughed. It sounded way too self-serving. "What I mean is that the grand opening is going to be great. And, yes, Gwen and Jesse have helped. But I put it all together and I'll tell you what—" she wasn't embarrassed when she looked his way and smiled "—I did a damned good job!"

"And I..." They were stopped at a red light and he shot her a smile. "I'm not the least bit surprised. You're an amazing woman."

"I am, aren't I?" Libby's laugh was as light as a feather. "Wait until you see it, Hal. The shelves are as neat as can be, and Gwen has arranged the yarn so that when you walk in the front door the colors take your breath away! We've got a spinner coming in to give a demonstration out on the front porch, and so many people have RSVP'd to say they were coming, including the arts-and-lifestyle editor for the *Plain Dealer*, the daily newspaper. They wouldn't have even known we exist except that I made all the right contacts."

"Like I said, amazing." They were nearing the Tremont neighborhood and Hal slowed down. Maybe he was reading Libby's mind; she didn't want the night to end either.

"We've got everything in place," she told Hal. "Including the roses you sent the other day. Can you believe they still look good?"

"Toss them." The light changed and he started up again. "There are more coming tomorrow. Yellow to put in the room with the lavender walls. And lavender to put in the room with the yellow walls."

"You shouldn't have."

"I wanted to." He slanted her a look. "Think all these flowers will help me score big points with that good lookin' woman who owns the shop?"

"What makes you think you haven't already?"

"Oh, yeah!" His voice was as sleek and content as his smile. "Exactly what I was hoping to hear."

"You're not holding it against me that I fought with my daughter last week?"

His lips pursed, Hal considered this. "Is there some kind of rule that mothers aren't supposed to argue with their daughters?"

"Of course not, but I—"

"Did what any other mother would have done. Any mother who gave a damn about her kid, at least. How's it going, by the way?"

Libby doubted if he saw her shrug. "We haven't said much

of anything to each other," she told him. "Maybe that's not so bad. At least we're not fighting."

This was a small thing but good, Libby knew. As she and Hal turned near the park and approached the shop, Libby felt a wave of contentment wash over her.

Until she saw that all the lights in the store were on.

"What on earth!" She sat up and peered out the window. They were still down the block and she couldn't make out much. But she did see shadows against the windows. There were people inside the store. Her imagination took off and panic enveloped her. "Police?" she asked. "Emergency crews? You don't suppose—"

She already had her hand on the door when Hal stopped her. "No police cars outside," he pointed out. "No ambulances or fire trucks." He slowed the car. The street outside the shop was filled with parked cars, and he cruised to a place across the street. Technically it wasn't a parking place, but technically the spots near the shop shouldn't have been full. Not at ten o'clock on a Thursday night.

Libby was out of the car before he punched the gearshift into Park. Hal was at her side before she was halfway across the street. Together, they hurried up the steps to the porch, and just as they got there the front door slammed open.

Loud rock blared from the stereo system where Libby kept only classical CDs. Kids spilled out of the doorway. One of them was a boy Libby didn't recognize. He was tall and broad and he had a beer bottle in his hand.

Meghan was right behind him.

"Out! Get out of here!" She pounded on the boy's back, but she was half his size and he was drunk. Not only didn't he feel it, he didn't care. Tears streamed down Meghan's cheeks. She stomped her feet. "All of you. Get out of here!" Meghan screamed, but the music was so loud nobody could have heard if they tried.

And nobody was trying.

There were kids sitting on the front counter, pounding the keys of the cash register. There were kids dancing in the front room. In the middle room Libby saw more kids. They were eating pizza while they chucked balls of yarn at each other, squealing when they got hit.

Stunned, Libby staggered back. At the same moment Meghan saw her.

Meghan's mouth fell open, and Libby froze, her insides twisted with anger, the disappointment she felt as real as a punch in the gut.

Through the whooshing noise of her blood against her ears, Libby heard Hal's grumbled curse. She watched him stride into the shop. A second later the music stopped.

"Everybody out!" Hal's voice thundered through the shop. There was a boy in the front room who looked to be no older than Meghan. He had just cracked the top off a bottle of beer. Hal yanked the bottle out of his hands, grabbed the boy by the scruff of the neck and chucked him onto the front porch. "I said out and I mean right now."

That was all it took it get everyone's attention. Kids dropped soda cans and handfuls of potato chips. They filed out the front door. Some of them were quiet and obviously embarrassed. They kept their eyes on the ground. Others didn't give a damn that they'd been caught and when they walked by, heads high and a gleam in their eyes, Libby forced herself to meet their gazes.

Most of the kids were strangers, but some Libby recognized, and even through the fog that filled her head she made sure she made note of who they were, who they were with and if there was any sign of them drinking. One of them was Tanya and she did her best to pretend she was invisible, refusing to meet Libby's eyes. Libby wasn't about to let the girl off so easily.

"I'll be calling your mother before I go to bed tonight," Libby promised, and Tanya blanched, hurried down the steps and disappeared in the direction of home. The last boy to walk out was wearing low-slung jeans, a baggy sweatshirt and a smile that just about begged somebody to dare to try to wipe it off his face. He had a skein of lace-weight alpaca yarn in his hands and he tossed it up and down.

One look at him and Libby's stomach soured. Given the slightest opportunity, she knew she would throw up. Instead, when he walked by, she raised her chin and held out her hand.

"Whatever," the boy grunted and just so she'd know returning the yarn was his idea and had nothing to do with the fire in her eyes, he chucked the skein at her.

Hal had already made a move to go after the boy when Libby grabbed his arm to stop him. It wasn't until she did that she realized she was shaking.

Hal knew it, too. It was the reason the anger in his eyes cooled. A wave of pain washed over his expression, mirroring what she was feeling inside. Rather than give in, she squeezed his arm in a way that told him she'd save breaking down for later and turned to face her daughter.

Meghan hadn't moved from the spot where Libby had last seen her. She was standing in front of the cash register, her hands clutched together at her waist.

"You want to tell me what happened here?" Libby's voice was icy. Strange, since her insides were on fire.

Meghan jumped as if she'd been slapped. The shock of seeing Libby wore off and she dissolved into tears. "I'm sorry. I'm so, so sorry." Her voice was high and tight. Once she started crying, she couldn't stop herself. She couldn't even stand. Her knees gave out, and she sank to the floor amidst a sprinkling of cigarette ash and potato chip crumbs. "I don't…I don't know how it happened. I asked Tanya and some of the kids to come over after Jesse left. Just a few kids, I swear. And then they brought their friends. And then more kids showed up. I didn't know them and I couldn't stop them. I'm sorry. I'm sorry."

Libby was sure she was. But that didn't mean she was going to forgive her easily. Or quickly. When she heard Hal close the front door behind her, she turned away from Meghan and dared a look around the shop.

The front room was in shambles. Books had been taken off the shelves and they were lying on the floor, open and with bent covers and torn pages. There were three pizza boxes balanced on top of the display of alpaca yarn Gwen had gone to such great lengths to arrange. The second room was in no better shape. Someone had made a noose out of yarn, and Mr. Bear—who Libby had just put back on display—was hanging from the ceiling light fixture. Someone else had scooped yarn off one of the display tables and piled it on the floor. Cushioned in the center of it was a case of beer.

Libby didn't bother to walk into the back room. Apparently someone thought it was really funny to shake a can of beer, then open it. From where she stood she could see beer running down the wall and polka-dotting the sock yarn.

Behind her, she heard Hal move to her side. She was trembling and she knew that with the slightest encouragement he would fold her into his arms and comfort her. She didn't have the luxury.

She turned to Meghan. "Get up and stop crying," she said. "Then go get a paper and pen."

From the tone of her voice, Meghan knew it was no use arguing and discussion was out of the question. Still sobbing, she pulled herself to her feet and walked behind the front counter.

Libby waited until she had the pen in her hands. "Now you're going to write down the name of every kid who was here and, if you know it, where they live and where they go to school. I want phone numbers, too."

Meghan blinked back tears. "But, Mom, you can't—"

"Can't what?" Libby moved so fast Meghan never saw her coming. She was at the front counter in an instant and she clutched it so hard her knuckles were white. "Don't tell me I can't call the parents of those kids. Because that's exactly what I intend to do. I'm going to call them. I'm going to tell them there was underage drinking going on here. I'm going to demand that each and every one of them talk to their children. And then you, Meghan Marie Cartwright, you are going to personally apologize—in writing—to every last one of them."

Meghan sniffed. She dared a glance at Hal, but seeing no support there, she looked back at the paper. "Can I do this upstairs?" she asked.

Libby blinked back the tears that threatened to dissolve her anger. "You can take it upstairs with you," she said. "But I want to find that list on the kitchen table when I get up there. Do you understand me?"

Meghan whisked the paper off the counter, scrambled around to the other side of it and hurried upstairs.

Once she was gone, Libby's shoulders slumped. She looked around and considered what to do next. It all might have been easier if she didn't feel as if the world had come crashing down around her.

"Where do you want to start?" Hal's question interrupted her thoughts.

"Start?" The chaos was overwhelming; she dropped her head into her hands. "There's no use even trying to do anything tonight," she said.

"Oh, come on, Lib." He couldn't have known, but he sounded so much like Rick had so many times that no matter what he was going to suggest, Libby knew she was going to reject it out of hand. "We're both running on some pretty high adrenaline. We'll get the worst of it cleaned up and—"

"No!" She hadn't meant to snap, not at Hal. He didn't deserve it. And besides, it simply wasn't fair. "I just need to fall over in a corner somewhere," she told him. "I'll get up early. I can make more progress when I'm not so upset or so exhausted. Right now it's too late to do anything."

"All right. I might not agree, but I understand. I'll be here at seven. I'm bringing the coffee and the guys from my shop, too, so get used to the idea. And Libby…" Hal cupped her face in one hand. "I'm going to kiss you, and just so you don't get any wrong ideas about what a lousy kisser I am, I want you to know this isn't how I pictured ending the night. I wanted to kiss you, all right. But not like this. Not like a buddy or a brother or something."

His kiss was as gentle as the brush of butterfly wings and as brief as the warmth that made Libby forget her problems— just for a moment.

When he was done, he turned and left.

Libby locked the door behind him. She stood with her

hands on the knob, her back braced against the front door for a few long minutes, looking at the mess, unable to comprehend what had gone on while she'd been out. Even as she watched, one of the pizza boxes set on top of the alpaca yarn sagged. Grease seeped through the cardboard and dripped onto the yarn.

"Damn." Libby raced forward. Just as she grabbed the box, it disintegrated. Mozzarella cheese and tomato sauce leaked through the bottom and all over the yarn. Bits of onion rained down along with black olives and green peppers.

Disgusted, Libby threw the box onto the floor. She made an attempt to wipe the onion off the yarn, but the more she wiped, the more she spread the tomato sauce. Pretty soon, what had been a minor stain on the yarn was a major one. Libby snapped.

"Damn, damn, damn!" She swept her arm over the display, scattering yarn and mozzarella cheese on the floor, and once it was there, she kicked it across the room. She pounded the nearest table with her fists, kicked a how-to knitting book and sent it skittering into the next room. She collapsed under the weight of her responsibilities and her dashed hopes.

"It's too late," she moaned. She slumped against the front counter and sat on the floor, her chin on her knees. "It's too late to do anything."

Like the echo of thunder, the words smashed into her. Familiar, and not because it was what she'd just said to Hal.

"It's too late." Libby dropped her head on her knees and

closed her eyes. It was no wonder the words were familiar. She'd used them before. The last time she'd felt this terrible, this hopeless.

The last time she'd seen her mother.

CHAPTER 13

"Go out and greet your guests. I'm fine. I'm ready. I don't need any more help." One hand on Grandpa Palmer's shoulder, the other brushing away Grandma P, who was trying—again—to adjust Libby's veil, she encouraged them to head for the door. "I'll be fine until Heather gets here. Honest!"

"I don't know." Wearing a blush-pink suit and a showy orchid the same silvery color as her hair, Grandma P was as pretty as a picture. She looked around the room in St. Paul's Cathedral, where generations of brides had waited for their big moment of walking down the aisle, and shook her head, disgusted. "Whoever heard of a maid of honor being late for a wedding? I told you from the start, that girl is cockamamy. Her head's always in the clouds."

"That's one of the things I like about Heather. It's why she's been my best friend for years." Libby laughed. "Besides, it's not her head that's the problem, it's the zipper in her gown. She's getting it fixed, so don't worry. The wedding can't get started without me, and I'm not going to budge from this room until Heather gets here." Libby tried another nudge, but she should have known it wasn't going to work. Grandma P didn't do anything Grandma P didn't want to do.

Grandpa P, on the other hand, looked as if, given half the chance, he would not only have left the room but the building, the church grounds and possibly the city.

"All these rich folks." Grandpa talked about the wealthy the way he used to talk about management before he retired from his job at the steel mill. As if they were some different species. No doubt he would have been much more relaxed if Rick's family and friends had presented their union cards at the door of the church. "Not much I can say to them. And not much they'd want to say to me."

"That's where you're wrong." Libby gave him a smile. This was the first time he'd ever worn a tux, and he looked handsome—and as uncomfortable as anyone Libby had ever seen. "You're the grandfather of the bride," she said. "That makes you the host of this shindig. And the guy who's going to walk me down the aisle. So go on out there and meet and greet. Before you know it, everyone in this church is going to be your friend.

"Come on, Grandpa." Because he wasn't moving, Libby wrapped her arm through his and led him to the door. He smelled like Old Spice instead of the Aqua Velva he always wore on Sundays, a sure sign he considered the day special. "Get out there and be your charming self."

Grandpa smiled. "You sure you're going to be okay?"

"I'm going to be more than okay."

"Yeah." Grandpa's eyes were misty. He kissed her cheek. "You are, princess. I'll see you out in the vestibule."

Grandma P kissed her, too, and reminded Libby as she had so many times in the years she was growing up that she was her special girl. When they left and closed the door behind them, Libby glanced at herself in the mirror. She did look like a princess, if she did say so herself, and she smoothed a hand over the gown that cost her a month's salary and was worth every penny. She touched up her lipstick and checked the clock that hung over the door. To calm her nerves, she paced the room and reminded herself that, nerves or not, this was going to be the most wonderful day of her life.

Her white satin pumps were silent against the plush carpeting, but her gown made a lovely swishy noise. Maybe because she was so busy listening to it—and the nervous thrumming of her heart—she didn't hear the door to the bride's room open.

When she flipped around to walk the other way, there was a woman standing at the door.

She was dressed in a dark suit and carrying a big box wrapped in silver-and-white paper. The bow on it was so huge, Libby couldn't see the woman's face.

"Rick's side, right?" Libby put on her best smile and hurried over to the door. "I don't think the ushers are seating anyone yet. If you'd like to wait—"

"Hello, Libby." The woman reached one hand over the box and flattened the bow. She was a stranger.

And she was looking at Libby as if they were old friends.

"Hi." Libby felt her smile fade. Unwilling to offend a woman who, for all she knew, was about to become a relative by marriage, she slapped it back into place. "You don't want to go into the church and be seated?"

"Not yet." The woman ran her tongue over her lips. "You don't know who I am, do you, Libby Lou?"

She hadn't. Not until the woman said the familiar nickname.

Libby sucked in a breath. It caught in her throat, and she was sure that her heart stopped along with it. Her arms close to her sides, her knees suddenly rubbery, she froze six feet away from her mother.

It had been years and, honestly, if Libby had passed Barb on the street, she never would have recognized her. She knew only the woman her memory had conjured, and that woman was part Janis Joplin—long haired and stoned—and part Wicked Witch of the West.

The Barb who stood in front of her was neither, and trying to reconcile reality with memory, Libby looked her over. Barb was petite and well dressed in a black suit and sensible pumps. Her only concession to nonconformity was the lacy shawl that was thrown over her shoulders. It was the same color as the rosy lipstick she'd nearly bitten away. Her hair was short and stylish, her makeup perfect.

"I know I wasn't invited," Barb said. "But I thought...." Though it was clear she would have been more comfortable looking anywhere else, it was just as clear she couldn't take her eyes off her daughter. "You're beautiful! You look like a princess."

It was so much like what Libby had heard from Grandpa P, it snapped her out of her shock.

Libby cleared her throat. "How did you—"

"Know where you were? That was easy. Your Rick, he comes from quite a prominent family. Your engagement announcement, then your wedding announcement—they were in all the papers. I still know people here in Pittsburgh. Word gets around."

"Then you don't—" Libby stopped herself before she could fully form the question. There was no use sounding too eager. Barb had had nearly twenty years to fill in the blanks of her life for Libby. She hadn't bothered.

Question or no question, Barb knew what Libby was going to ask her. "I don't live here in Pittsburgh," she said. "Not anymore. I left after—" Her fingers fidgety, Barb straightened the bow on the package. "I live in Cleveland now. I have my own yarn shop. Barb's Knits. Maybe someday you can come see it."

"Maybe." It was a better answer than the one Libby was tempted to give. *Why would I want to? Why would I care? Do you honestly think I'll drop everything and come, just because you showed up out of nowhere and—*

If there was one thing Libby valued it was reason. Never more so than today, when her nerves were stretched to the fraying point. The questions she longed to ask would get her nowhere, so she gathered her composure and tamped down her emotions.

"You didn't come all the way here just to invite me to your yarn shop," she told Barb.

"No. I didn't." Barb had been toeing an invisible line between the doorway and the rest of the room. She crossed it and set the box she was carrying on a nearby table. "When I saw your engagement announcement…well, I always dreamed of making something special for you for your wedding." She stepped back to allow Libby to open the box, and when Libby eyed it as if there might be a snake inside, Barb managed a thin smile.

Only the top of the box was wrapped and the ribbon didn't go all the way around it. Barb lifted off the top and pushed aside the tissue paper. Inside was an exquisite bedspread knit from delicate white cotton. "It's called a counterpane," Barb said. "It's made up of small squares, and every four squares are joined to make a bigger square. The pattern is called Mountain Lace. It's old. From the 1800s. The pattern, not the counterpane." Barb's laugh was short-lived. "It's a special present for a special day. For a special girl."

Again Barb echoed her grandparents' words.

Again Libby felt a thread of uneasiness coil through her.

She twitched it away, but even that couldn't get rid of the seed Barb had planted. In Libby's mind, she pictured what would happen if Grandma and Grandpa P ran into Barb out of the blue. On a day that should have been as special for them as it was for Libby—a day when they shouldn't have had a thing to worry about but having a good time—it would come as a shock.

"Are you going to let Grandma and Grandpa P know you're here?"

"I don't think that's a good idea. Last time we saw each other…well…things didn't go very well. I couldn't—"

"Then why did you come here?"

This, too, was a question Barb wasn't expecting. Or maybe it was the edge of acerbity in Libby's voice that surprised her. Heaven knew, it surprised Libby, too.

She thought about apologizing, then changed her mind. There wasn't time. And besides, she wasn't sure she was sorry.

"I know you're not happy to see me," Barb replied, before Libby had time to say anything.

"I'm not unhappy. I'm not happy, either." Until that moment, Libby didn't realize that she was rubbing the satin edging on her veil. She dropped it before she could do any damage. "I'm just surprised you bothered."

"I can't say I blame you. It's been a long time. But just so you know…" Barb stepped forward, and for one heart-stopping moment Libby thought her mother was going to hug her. Logic dictated that she resist. But in her heart Libby knew that, given half the chance, she'd melt into her mother's arms.

In the years that followed, Libby thought about what had happened next a thousand times. Each time, she wondered what she could have done differently. What she should have done to keep from looking like a fool. But every time the memory played like a video inside her head, the results were the same.

Desperate for some proof of her mother's affection, Libby darted forward to hug her.

Barb held back.

And Libby found herself floundering and alone.

Regret, searing and painful, shone in Barb's eyes. Still, she didn't move. She swallowed hard. "I want you to know that there hasn't been a day that's gone by that I haven't thought of you," she said.

It was the perfect opportunity for Libby to tell Barb that she understood, but nearly twenty years of loneliness made empathy impossible. And the lost opportunity to feel her mother's arms around her left her cold.

Libby raised her chin. "You have a really funny way of showing it."

If Libby's honesty surprised Barb, it was only for a moment. The next second, her shoulders shot back. When she spoke, her voice wasn't chilly, not like Libby's. It sizzled with emotion and burned with anger. "Damn it, Libby, it's not like I haven't tried. All these years, I tried to see you, to get in touch with you. Your grandparents—"

"Don't even try to make it sound like this is their fault. Grandma and Grandpa P only want what's best for me. It's all they've ever wanted. They love me. It's more than you were ever willing to do."

Barb opened her mouth to respond, then snapped it shut again. The emotion that burned in her eyes flickered. It died. "You're right," she said. She backed toward the door. "There's nothing I can do to change any of that. Not now. And there's nothing I can do to prove to you that things might have been different. Not on my own. One person can only go so far. It takes the other person to meet them halfway. Maybe every time you see that counterpane—"

Libby didn't give her a chance to finish. She jammed the top back on the box and shoved the package into Barb's hands. "The best present you can give me," she said, "is to stay out of my life."

There were tears on Barb's cheeks. One arm cradling the box, she opened the door with her free hand and stepped into the hallway. "I love you, Libby," she said.

"It's too late for that." If Barb couldn't see that, then Libby had to point it out. "It's too late to do anything."

"It's too late."

The words echoed at Libby and shook her from the past. There was a paper napkin on the floor—just part of the mess that filled Metropolitan Knits—and she grabbed it and swiped it under her nose. The grand opening was scheduled for the next day and the store was a disaster. It was too late to get started on cleaning any of it, and it wouldn't have mattered anyway. No one person could even begin to make a dent in everything that needed to be done.

Given half a chance and a moment's notice, she'd chuck the whole idea of owning her own business and the ridiculous notion that she could actually make her own way in the world and go back to Pittsburgh to live in the shadow of Rick and Belinda's happy marriage and their new family.

But none of it was nearly as bad as thinking that Meghan had turned her back on every scrap of common sense Libby had ever taught her and every bit of love Libby had always offered with her whole heart.

The wreckage was so complete, the situation so hopeless, it was no wonder her mind was desperate to glom onto something—anything—else.

Too bad what it decided to focus on was that one last time she'd seen Barb.

"Damn." Libby pulled herself to her feet. She threw away a piece of pizza that had been left on top of the cash register and an empty can of beer that had been tossed under the front counter.

"I had the chance," Libby mumbled to herself. She wadded up another napkin and pitched it. "I had the chance to reach out to her, to build a bridge. Instead…" Her shoulders rose and fell.

Maybe things could have been different.

It was that thought more than anything that ate away at Libby's composure. Maybe if she hadn't spoken to Barb so harshly, if she hadn't let Barb walk out that door…

There was nothing like regret to make a bad situation even worse.

And there was nothing she could do about it.

Or was there?

One person can only go so far. It takes the other person to meet them halfway.

Barb's words cut through Libby's dark thoughts. There was nothing she could do now to meet her mother halfway. But maybe she could do the next best thing, and somehow by doing it, maybe she could make things right with Barb.

By the time she decided it was a good idea, she was already dialing the phone. She was talking even before Jesse had a chance to ask what the hell was wrong with her for calling so late.

"You know what happened on the day I got married, don't you?" Libby blurted out. She didn't wait for Jesse to answer. He and Barb had been soul mates. Of course she'd told him what had happened at the church.

"She said it," Libby went on, "and I wouldn't listen. She told me no one person can do things alone. She told me I had to reach out, and I didn't. I thought I could carry the load myself."

There was silence on the other end of the line, and for a moment she thought Jesse had decided she had really lost her mind and hung up.

Finally she heard him clear his throat. "I know what happened at the shop," he said. "Hal called and told me. But, Libby, you're not talking about the store, are you?"

"No." She was crying. And laughing. "It's not the store I need help with," she said, then added, "Okay, yes, I do need help with the store. Huge amounts of help. But that's not what I'm talking about. She gave me the opportunity, Jesse. The opportunity to get to know her. I blew it. I'm so sorry. Things could have been different. If I wasn't so dead set on proving it was all her fault, I could have loved her."

She didn't have to see Jesse to know what he was doing. As he always did when he was considering something important, he would be nodding. He'd scratch a finger behind his ear.

"You know," he said, "it's never too late."

CHAPTER 14

Twenty-four hours earlier, Libby never would have believed it was possible—the grand opening was officially under way. The store was filled with music, candlelight and plenty of people and, wonder of wonders, everything was perfect. There was no sign of the chaos from the night before, and looking around, the transformation both exhilarated and humbled her.

Neither emotion came as much of a surprise. The help she'd gotten from Gwen, Hal and mostly Jesse was enough to make her believe in the very real—and very potent—power of friendship. And the fact that Hal's employees, along with Tanya's parents—who said it was the least they could do to apologize for their daughter's behavior—had pitched in with enthusiasm made Libby think there was still hope for Metropolitan Knits. Even Peg from the beauty shop next door had shown up that morning, a mop in one hand and a bucket in the other. She'd heard the commotion the night before, and though she hadn't been willing to stick her nose where it didn't belong and call the police, she knew something was wrong and was willing to help set it right again.

Except for Meghan being too quiet and that Libby had yet to find the words to explain her disappointment without sounding accusatory and, so, had said little in return, things were going better than she could ever have imagined. Maybe Hal knew that's what she was thinking when he walked by her as she was chatting with the arts editor from the local paper and gave her a wink.

Then again, maybe her new wine-colored pantsuit—and the stylish and gorgeous wrap Gwen had knitted to go with it—was working its magic. Libby glanced around at the crowd gathered in Metropolitan Knits and smiled.

"Yes," she said in response to the reporter's last question. "Knitting is more popular than ever. Some people don't understand why."

"But—let me guess—you do?" The reporter was an eager-beaver type, fresh out of college and mystified by what he'd called "a woman's hobby" when he'd first walked in. Clearly he looked down on anything he considered homey or hand-crafted and expected her to come up with some answer that was perfectly sweet and predictable.

"It's all about process," Libby said instead, and from the way he paused, his pen poised over his notebook, she knew she'd caught him off guard. "Knitting has a relaxing, Zenlike quality. It's meditation. And it's prayer. It's therapy. Ask knitters what's more important, a finished garment or the process of knitting that garment, and my bet is that most of them will tell you that it's the actual physical act of knitting that appeals to them. Often it doesn't matter what they make. Or even if they finish a project. It's the process that's important because it's what anchors them and grounds them. It's what frees their minds. Their creative spirits just naturally follow."

"And that's why you knit? Because of this meditation thing? You mean you go into a sort of trance while you work?"

Libby went into a trance while she knitted, all right. A trance of pure panic accented by frequent mistakes, dropped stitches and a lot of—but not as often lately—total confusion.

None of which she was about to admit to a newspaper reporter.

"No trances," she said and she smiled because though the reporter didn't know it, Hal was standing right behind him and giving Libby the thumbs-up. "Just relaxation. That's what it's all about. As a matter of fact…" Susan and Cecilia, two of the women Libby had met at Meet the Teacher Night at Meghan's school and who had since become good and loyal customers, walked by, and Libby snagged them. "You're only going to hear a shop owner's side of the story from me. Talk to two real knitters. They'll be happy to fill you in."

Happy was putting it mildly. The last Libby saw of them, Susan and Cecilia had the reporter sandwiched between them. They were talking his ear off while they showed him around the shop.

"That was slick." Hal grinned and handed Libby a glass of champagne.

"You think?" She took the glass but dared only a tiny sip. The party had just started, and she couldn't take the chance of not being on top of her game. She was party planner and hostess, proprietor and official greeter. She didn't have time for indulgence. Even when that indulgence was Hal and the glint in his eyes told her he would have liked nothing better than to have her alone in a quiet corner.

"It's working out well." She didn't need to tell him; he could see it for himself. Maybe she just needed the reassurance of putting it into words. "I couldn't have done it without you. And your employees. If any of them ever want to take knitting lessons—"

The look of horror on Hal's face said it all. "They'd tie my legs together and toss me in the lake if I ever even suggested it. They didn't mind helping."

"Because you told them they had to help."

"There wasn't all that much for us to do by the time we got here this morning. You and Jesse must have worked like dogs last night. Why didn't you let me stick around to help?"

A shrug wasn't a good enough answer, but since Libby couldn't find the words, it would have to do. "Jesse's a great guy." Like the night he'd come over for dinner, Jesse was dressed to the nines for the party. In dark pants and a pine-green sweater that Barb had made, he looked distinguished. Since he wasn't the sociable type, Libby hadn't asked him to do any of the meeting or greeting. He was standing just inside the doorway of the kitchen showroom, watching the action, in charge of making sure there was plenty of ice. Although he didn't touch a drop himself, he volunteered to open wine and champagne bottles, and when one bottle was empty, he got rid of it and put another in its place.

"Funny how the past can show up in the present. Even when you're not expecting it." Libby's voice was as thoughtful as the look she cast Jesse's way. "You think Barb knew it would turn out this way?"

"You think that's why she left you the store?"

"I think she knew I longed for a family, someone besides Grandma and Grandpa P. I think she knew that with Jesse and Gwen…" Gwen knew everyone who walked through the front door. Even as Libby watched, she hugged a longtime customer and piloted the woman over to a display of recycled silk. A pang tightened Libby's chest. "Barb must have been a pretty smart lady."

As quickly as the contentment welled up in her, it passed away. Though Libby had insisted that Meghan come down and join the festivities, she couldn't make her participate. When Jesse walked by with two newly opened bottles of champagne, she saw Meghan slip from the classroom into the kitchen. She didn't look any happier now than she had when the party started.

"You should probably go talk to her." Since Hal's suggestion echoed what Libby was thinking, she wasn't about to argue. She handed him her champagne glass and went in search of her daughter.

She found Meghan sitting at the desk in the corner of the kitchen Libby used as an office.

"Hey!" Libby tried her best to keep her voice light. "Why aren't you out there partying? It's going really well."

"Great." Meghan kicked the tile floor with the toe of her sneakers.

"Of course it's great. That means the word is getting out. The store is a success."

"And that means we'll never leave."

It was a subject Libby thought had long been put to rest. "Is that what you want to do? Leave?"

"What do you think?"

"I think…." Libby drew in a breath and let it out slowly. "I think we've had a tough time these past few weeks. I think we have a lot to talk about. And you have a lot to do to pay me back for the yarn that was damaged by your friends." They had talked about this earlier in the day and Meghan knew Libby wasn't going to give an inch. Maybe that's why she shot her mother a look of disgust.

"It's just stupid yarn."

"It's my stupid yarn. And it's stupid yarn that will help pay for your college education one of these days. When I have to throw it away, it's like tossing money out the window. You understand, don't you?"

"Do you understand that I hate it here?"

"I'm sorry." Libby reached for her daughter and would

have patted her shoulder if Meghan didn't slip out from under her hand.

It would have been easy to fight, but if Libby had learned anything since thinking about her wedding day it was that even when an argument was appropriate, it wasn't always for the best.

"Look...." Meghan was still sitting at the desk, and Libby bent to look her in the eye. "Maybe you'll have more fun if you get involved in what's going on. You could meet our customers."

"A bunch of old ladies who like to knit. Boring."

Libby spoke through gritted teeth. "Then I'll tell you what...." There was an empty platter nearby and she handed it to Meghan. "The caterer left extra cheese upstairs in the fridge. It's all cut up in little cubes. Fill the plate and add some crackers. Since you're grounded and can't leave the house, that will give you something to do."

Meghan took the dish out of her hands. "Is having something to do supposed to make me feel better about the way you embarrassed me in front of my friends last night?"

"You didn't look embarrassed," she reminded her daughter, and the no-nonsense tone of her voice must have finally made Meghan realize she was done trying to be reasonable; Meghan refused to meet Libby's eyes. "You looked like you wanted them to leave. You couldn't get them to do it, so Hal and I had to."

"And then you had to call their parents." Meghan dragged

herself out of the chair and headed over to the stairs that led up to the apartment. "They're never going to talk to me again."

"The ones who feel like that aren't worth being friends with."

"Oh, yeah." Meghan stomped to the stairs. "That makes me feel way better."

Enough was enough, and Libby had reached her limit. She put a hand on Meghan's shoulder and spun her around. "Listen up, young lady, it's not my job to make you feel better. It's not my goal in life, either. I'm your mother, and that means I'm here to make sure you grow up healthy and smart and strong. If you don't like that—"

"I don't."

"Then maybe you need to rethink your view of the world. It doesn't revolve around you, Meghan. It's about time you grew up and realized that."

Meghan opened her mouth, but it was clear that she knew if she said a word she was going to be in more trouble than ever. Rather than risk it, she turned and ran upstairs.

Libby pulled in a calming breath, scrubbed her hands over her face and vowed to talk to Meghan more later. Right now she had other responsibilities, and a store full of people to attend to.

According to the press releases she'd sent to local media, the grand opening was scheduled from six to nine. By ten, the party was still going strong, and Libby wasn't about to hurry people along. Loyal clients had heard the shop had reopened and had shown up in droves, along with many of the new customers Libby had cultivated. They complimented her on her choice of yarn and many of them took advantage of the products Libby had put on special sale. By the time eleven o'clock rolled around and the last of her guests was out the door, the total on the cash register proved it was her best day of sales ever.

"I'm exhausted." Libby finished counting out the register, filled out a deposit slip for the day's receipts and looked over to where Gwen was collecting used plates and cups.

"Leave it," she told her. "I'll get it in the morning. For now…" She saw Jesse cleaning up the wine bottles and she waved him over. Hal was outside helping the spinner load her equipment into her van, and Libby waited until he came back in. She poured three glasses of wine and a cup of coffee for Jesse.

"I want to propose a toast," she said. "To all of us. To all of you. We made it happen and—" She peeked into the classroom and the back showroom. "Where's Meghan?"

Hal shook his head. Jesse shrugged. "Saw her earlier," Gwen said. "She was sitting in the classroom."

Libby thought back to her argument with Meghan. "That was a really long time ago," she said. "She must be upstairs."

Before Libby could make a move, Jesse was already on his way. He was gone too long, and when he came back, Meghan wasn't with him.

"Not in the apartment," he said. "Or up in her new room.

I found this in the kitchen, though." He showed Libby the platter she'd sent Meghan upstairs to fill. It was empty. "This was on it." He held up Meghan's cell phone. Wherever she was, the message was clear—she didn't want her mother to be able to find her.

Anger shot through Libby, and though she didn't mean to take it out on Jesse, she was already brushing past him. "Are you sure you looked? Everywhere?"

"Everywhere." He put a hand on her arm to stop her. "Twice in the attic. I think maybe her backpack's gone, too. At least I didn't see it up at the top of the stairs where she usually drops it."

"And outside?"

"I'm on it." Hal was out the door before Libby could move that way.

"I'll check the basement." Gwen raced for the back of the store.

Libby was fairly certain that checking every inch of the store, the upstairs apartment and the attic again wasn't going to help. But it gave her something to do, and right then, doing something was better than letting her anger get the best of her. By the time she was back down in the store, Gwen was standing near the cash register and Hal had just returned from outside.

"You're not going to like this," Hal said.

"I already don't like it." Libby squeezed her eyes shut and fought for control. "Tell me."

"Peg, at the beauty shop." Hal scraped a hand over his chin. "Good thing she's so nosy. She says she was watching out the window and saw Meghan get into a car. There was a boy behind the wheel. He had a long, dark ponytail, and she says she thinks he was one of the kids who was here in the store last night."

"And we don't know his name." Libby knew there had to be a calculated, reasonable way to handle the situation. If she wasn't so angry at Meghan for going out when she'd been told not to, she actually might have found it.

"How about Tanya?" The suggestion came from Hal, and Libby couldn't have been more grateful. She went for the phone and didn't bother with Tanya. She talked to Mrs. Pruitt, who was still mad enough at her daughter for what had gone on the night before to make Tanya talk.

"His name is Mike Moreno," Libby said, hanging up the phone. "According to Mrs. Pruitt, Tanya's not sure where he goes to school, but she knows where he lives. Over on West Fourteenth. In those apartments near the freeway exit."

Hal was out the door in a flash, and Libby didn't have to ask where he was going.

Her heart in her throat and her stomach tied in knots, all she could do was wait.

"I'm going to have to call Rick."

Libby waited for someone to tell her she was wrong. Of course, she wasn't and she knew it. If either Gwen or Hal told her she was, she would have known they were just trying to placate her. Rather than put them in that position and make them uncomfortable, she excused herself and went upstairs to the apartment to make the call.

It was nearly two in the morning, and Rick had been sound asleep. He wasn't happy about being woken up.

"It's kind of late to chat, don't you think?" he asked.

Thinking of everything she'd learned from Hal, Libby cut to the chase. "It's Meghan," she said.

"What?" In an instant the sleepiness was gone from Rick's voice. "What about Meghan? Is she hurt? Is she—"

"She ran away."

His stunned silence proved it was the last thing he'd expected. But then, that wasn't a surprise. Libby had never dreamed anything like this would happen either. Not to her daughter. "I thought maybe..." She'd hoped to show Rick that she had the situation under control, so she bit back her tears. "I thought maybe she might be there with you."

"Here? Wait a minute! Back up, Lib." Apparently he'd woken Belinda, because he held the phone away from his mouth and said, "It's Meghan. She ran away," before he got back to his conversation. "How do you know—"

"Hal talked to Mike," she said and knew she had to explain. "Mike is a friend of Meghan's."

"Meghan's been seeing a boy? Are you crazy? She's only fourteen!"

That was an argument for another day. For now, all that

mattered was finding Meghan. Finding her safe. "Mike, this friend of Meghan's, he picked her up here about seven-thirty. He says he drove her to the bus station."

"And where did he say she was going?"

"He claims he doesn't know. He says she refused to talk about it. I believe him, Rick. Hal, the friend who spoke to Mike, was plenty angry and he says that this Mike kid isn't nearly as tough and as cool as he likes to pretend. If Mike knew anything, he would have spilled his guts. Mike says he dropped Meghan off at the bus station downtown and she went inside. Jesse's over there now looking for her, but he hasn't called, so I know he hasn't found her. I thought...I thought you should know."

"You're damned right." It wasn't often Rick let his temper get out of control. "If you didn't care more about that yarn shop than you do about your daughter—"

"That's not fair, Rick, and you know it. I've tried to do my best for Meghan. Always. I've put her first and myself last. I can't help it that she walked out of here."

"She walked out because you weren't watching her."

"She's fourteen, and maybe rebellion is part of the package, I don't know. I do know that it's not fair to lay the guilt trip solely on me. She learned a whole lot about being immature and selfish from you. And while we're at it, we might as well throw in irresponsible, too. Only an egotist would put his own instant gratification over the welfare of his family."

"I have my own happiness to worry about."

"And that about puts it in a nutshell, doesn't it? You have yourself to worry about, and the hell with everyone else."

"If this is about how I chose Belinda over you—"

"It isn't." Libby was sure of it and the conviction rang in her voice. "This is about nothing and no one except Meghan." Worry clawed at Libby's insides, and this time when she started to cry, she didn't care if Rick knew it. "I want her back, Rick. I want to know she's safe."

"I know." The severity of the situation hit, and Rick drew in a shaky breath. "I'll call some of Meghan's friends here," he said. "I'll let you know what I find out. Don't worry, Lib, she's going to be okay. We're going to find her."

It wasn't until she hung up the phone that Libby realized Hal had come up to the apartment. He was standing in the doorway between the kitchen and the dining room.

"I told Gwen to go home," he said. "There's really nothing else she can do here tonight. And Jesse called. Nobody at the bus station remembers seeing Meghan, but that doesn't mean much. The shift changed at eleven. If she bought a ticket before then—"

"A kid shouldn't be allowed to buy a ticket. Not when she's alone. There should be some law against that, shouldn't there?"

Hal knew she didn't really expect an answer. He walked into the living room and took Libby in his arms.

Then again, maybe that was the only answer she really needed.

CHAPTER 15

Hal and Libby sat on the couch in the living room, his arm around her shoulders while she alternately cried and worried.

He didn't offer clichés in the hopes of comforting her, and for that she was grateful. He held her and he listened. And when the sun was just beginning to brighten the sky and the phone rang and Libby answered, he closed his fingers around hers, sending her strength without saying a word.

"Lib, it's me."

"Rick?" Her heart in her throat, Libby sat up. "Have you heard? Is she—"

"She's here. In Cranberry. She's fine, Lib. She's safe. She showed up at the front door a couple minutes ago. She took a cab from the bus station in Pittsburgh."

"Oh." Her response was anticlimactic to say the least, but it was the only thing Libby could manage to choke out. She twined her fingers through Hal's, and instinctively he knew the news was good. He smiled.

"Can I talk to her?" she asked Rick.

His laugh wasn't lighthearted. "I'm not sure this is a good

time," he said. "The first thing I did when I saw her was give her a hug and a kiss. Then I read her the riot act. She's in the kitchen crying her eyes out and saying she's sorry. I'm going to let her suffer for a while, then give her a cup of cocoa and send her to bed. Sound like a good plan to you?"

Libby's throat clogged. She cleared it with a cough. "Rick, before you tuck her into bed, give her a kiss for me, will you?"

He assured her he would and hung up.

"She's okay." Libby laughed. She cried. She fell into Hal's arms. "She's all right, Hal. She went to Pittsburgh. She's with Rick. She's okay!"

Relief cannonballed through her, and Libby couldn't think of a better way to celebrate than with a kiss. In one pristine moment of unadulterated joy, her lips met Hal's. One moment extended to two, the kiss deepened and his arms tightened around her.

Libby didn't resist. She didn't even consider it. This was a new day and a new beginning. She was no fool. Just because Meghan was safely with Rick didn't mean their problems were solved or their troubles were over. But for now, her daughter's safety was all she could ask for.

"Hey!" Hal put his hands on her shoulders and nudged her far enough back to look into her eyes. There was a grin on his lips. It glinted in his eyes. "This isn't some kind of thank-you sex, is it? I mean, you're not just feeling all warm and fuzzy because I sat here all night with you?"

"You got a problem with it if it is?"

He considered for a moment. His smile got wider.

Libby slipped off the couch and tugged Hal to his feet. When she took him to her bedroom, his smile was broader than ever.

"Meghan's going to stay in Pittsburgh the rest of the weekend and maybe on into next week." The next day, Libby hung up from an early-afternoon phone call with Meghan and told Hal what had happened. "She says her father will call the school and see if he can get her excused for a couple days. I think she's going to tell me that she wants to live with Rick and Belinda."

Hal had just poured a cup of coffee for Libby. He came up behind her, deposited the cup on the table in front of her and wrapped his arms around her. "How do you feel about that?"

She shrugged. She was wearing the purple satin robe Rick had bought her for their fifteenth wedding anniversary, and when her shoulders rose and fell, Hal's hands skimmed her arms. Just as it had all through the early-morning hours, his touch ignited her desires. She promised herself she'd give in to the temptation later.

"I know nothing's written in stone," Libby said. "I realize Meghan has to take some time and think things over. But I'll admit, if she chooses to live there, I'll be hurt. She says Belinda and Rick are cooler and hipper and life with them isn't nearly as boring as it is here."

Hal bent and kissed the nape of her neck. "Boring, huh? She hasn't been around these past couple hours!"

"And if she had been, the past couple hours would've been plenty boring," Libby reminded him. "You can't stay overnight, not when Meghan's around."

"Understood." He nodded, and when Libby stood, he reached for the belt that cinched the robe around her waist. "But when she's not here…"

"When she's not here, I've still got a shop to run." She kissed Hal's cheek. "I'll see you later."

"For dinner?"

"For dinner."

"And after?"

Though she tried to look somber, it was impossible not to blush. "After dinner," she told him, "we'll have dessert."

The next three days—and nights—were incredible. Hal was an enthusiastic and considerate lover, and for the first time in as long as she could remember, Libby felt pretty and sexy.

He stayed the night, and in the morning it was nice to find him smiling at her from the pillow next to hers. He came to the shop after work each evening and brought her flowers, and took her to dinner and treated her like a queen.

It was enough to make any woman happy.

But even that wasn't nearly as wonderful as the call she finally got from Meghan. The one in which her daughter told her she wanted to return to Cleveland.

Libby met the news with as little emotion as she could.

After all they'd been through, this didn't seem to be the time for Meghan to hear her jumping up and down and shouting yahoo. "You're not having fun with Daddy and Belinda?"

"Yeah. Sort of." Libby didn't have to see Meghan to know she was kicking the toe of her shoe against the floor. "It's just that…I don't know, Mom. I like visiting Dad. And I like staying in my old room. And this morning Dad made pancakes. You know, like he always used to do for us."

"But…?"

"I dunno." Meghan sniffled and something told Libby another apology was in the offing. Meghan had already come to her senses and admitted that she'd acted out of anger when she'd run away. She knew what she'd done was wrong and inconsiderate, not to mention dangerous, and a dozen times in the last days she'd told Libby and Rick that she was sorry she'd put them through so much. They'd said all they needed to say about the subject. It was time for new beginnings.

Before she could remind Meghan of that, her daugnte went on. "As much as I like it here in Cranberry, Mom, it's not the same. Without you here, it's just not home."

"I miss you, too, sweetie."

"And you'll let me come back?"

"Of course!" Libby was crying and she didn't care if Meghan knew it. These were tears of joy. "Anytime. Right now, if you want to. I can hop in the car and be in Pittsburgh in a couple hours."

"Nah." Meghan sniffled. "Daddy says he'll bring me home tomorrow."

"On a Tuesday?" Libby was surprised. Rick didn't take care of personal business on workdays. "What time?"

"I'll be there for dinner," Meghan told her, and just as she did, Jesse walked into the store. By now, he must have been used to seeing Libby with tears in her eyes. He wasn't used to seeing her smiling at the same time, too, though.

"What's up?" he asked once she'd hung up.

"Meghan's coming home."

"Good." Jesse nodded. "I need some help if I'm going get that room of hers finished soon." He watched Libby reach for a tissue. "If you're happy, why are you crying?"

"I'm crying because I'm happy. And because—" she wiped the tears from her eyes "—since Meghan's been gone, I've missed her so much I can't even see straight. And then when I think about Barb and how she must have missed me…"

"Hey!" Jesse reached across the counter and squeezed her hand. "Doesn't matter anymore. Nothing we can do to change the past."

Libby sniffed and wiped her nose. "For all our problems, I guess I've raised a daughter who's a better person than me. Even Meghan is big enough to admit that what she did was wrong. I was never enough of a grown-up to tell Barb any of that. I'm sorry I never did. Maybe if I'd just taken the step, accepted her wedding gift, maybe things could have been different."

"Oh, I don't know. I think they already are." He patted her hand and went upstairs. He was back in a few minutes and carrying a big cardboard box.

"Found this when we were fixing up the attic," he said. "Thought I'd hold on to it for a while and sort of test the waters. You know, see if you were ready for it or not. Something tells me after that call from Her Majesty, maybe you are." He set the box on the floor, opened it and lifted out another box. This one was wrapped in silver-and-white paper that was brittle and tattered. The gossamer ribbon on it was smashed and dusty, but Libby would have recognized it anywhere.

"She kept it." She came around to the front of the counter. "All these years, Barb kept my wedding gift."

"And I know she would want you to have it." He put the box in her hands.

Libby lifted the cover on the package and looked at the delicate counterpane. It needed an airing and probably a good washing, too, but Gwen would know how to handle the bedspread without damaging the delicate fabric. "She said it was for new beginnings," she told Jesse. "I guess this counts, huh? And speaking of that…"

Libby hadn't told anyone what she was planning. Not even Hal. But now didn't seem the time to keep secrets.

"I called Al Zelinsky," she told Jesse. "You know, the sign painter."

"Sure." Jesse's curiosity was piqued. "Something wrong

with the new sign? I hope not. Al, he's dependable. If he screwed up—"

"He did. Absolutely." Libby nodded solemnly. "He forgot to add something very important to our name. I'm having him stop by this afternoon to remove the sign. Then he can make the changes."

"Changes?" Jesse scratched a hand through his short-cropped hair.

"Yeah, I'm changing the name of the shop to Barb's Metropolitan Knits. What do you think of that?"

Jesse didn't answer. In fact, he didn't say a thing. He just smiled.

There were fresh flowers on Barb's grave. Libby knew who'd left them there, and rather than remove the roses from the in-ground vase next to the headstone, she set the bouquet she'd brought with her near where Barb's name was carved in granite.

"Wish you could have met your grandmother," she told Meghan. A cold wind blew across the rolling hills of Lake View Cemetery and she scooted closer to her daughter.

"Yeah, I guess I wish I could have met her, too. Jesse says she was cool."

"She was very cool."

Meghan was huddled into a peacoat that had been too big the winter before. Now the sleeves were above her wrists. Libby's little girl was growing up. She looked over her shoulder toward where Hal was waiting near the car and signalled to him that they'd be done in a minute. Before they could move, though, Megan spoke.

"I've got something to give you," she said. She'd brought her backpack with her and she lifted it off the ground and cradled it. "I was going to wait until we got home, but I told Jesse and he said this might be better. I dunno." She wrinkled her nose, and for a moment she looked exactly like the little girl Libby used to read bedtime stories to each night.

Meghan unzipped her backpack and pulled out a stack of envelopes four inches high. The bundle was tied with a piece of purple yarn.

"I found them," Meghan said. "In the attic."

"Which explains why they look a little dirty." Libby wrinkled her nose. "Whatever it is, are you sure you want to keep them?"

"They're not mine. They're for you, Mom." Meghan pushed the pile into her hands. "Every one of them. They're addressed to you." She pointed to the envelope at the top of the stack. "When you used to live with Grandma and Grandpa P. They're from Barb."

Libby's heart clutched. She reached for the stack of envelopes and riffled through them. Some of the postmarks were still legible, and she saw that the dates corresponded with her birthdays and with various holidays. Every single one of them had *Return to sender* written on it in Grandpa's plain, blunt hand.

"All those years…" Libby looked down at the gravestone at her feet. "She tried to keep in touch. And all those years

Grandma and Grandpa sent her letters back. More wasted opportunities and lost possibilities." It was important for Meghan to understand the dynamics of the family relationship. "Everyone makes mistakes."

Meghan nodded. "That's what Jesse said."

"And you know that Barb kept sending the cards, even when they were all returned to her...you know that shows how much she loved me, right? The way all mothers love their daughters."

"Yup." Meghan put her hand in Libby's. "Jesse said that, too."

"So what do you think? We can start reading these in the car."

"I don't think so." Meghan was sure of herself. "I think this is something you need to do by yourself. Barb—Grandma—she meant those cards just for you."

"All right." Libby skirted around a standing headstone and over to the car. "Then what do you want to do when we get home?"

"I was kind of hoping..." Meghan kicked the toe of her sneaker against a tuft of grass. "I dunno, I've been watching and I guess it does kind of look like fun. I was kind of hoping you'd teach me how to knit."

Libby laughed and hugged Meghan to her. "I don't know, Meggie. I'm not much of a teacher. I think I can handle the casting on and the knit stitch. But if I ever have to knit two together..."

Libby's laughter broke the stillness. "Maybe," she told her daughter, "that's something we all need to learn together," and she walked to where Hal was waiting.

* * * * *

A Sweater for a Bear

Like people, teddy bears come in all shapes and sizes. This sweater fits my own personal bear, Tedda, given to me by my uncle, Ted Deka, one Christmas (I won't say how long ago that was!). Tedda is 15" tall and a svelte 11½" around the chest. The sweater is stylishly baggy on him. This simple pattern can be easily adapted to fit your own teddy. Because it's small and easy, it's a great way to try out color and stitch patterns, too.

Materials:
Worsted weight yarn (approx. 100 yards)
Size 8 knitting needles

Gauge:
Approx. 4 ½ stitches to the inch

Back:
CO 30.

Work in stockinette stitch (knit one row, purl one row) until piece measures 4¹/₂" from the beginning, ending with a purl row.

Next row, knit 10, bind off 10, knit last 10 stitches.

Work these last 10 stitches for four more rows, k2 together every other row at the neck edge.

Bind off stitches.

Add yarn to other shoulder and repeat.

Bind off all stitches.

Front:

Work the same way as the back until sweater measures 4".

Knit across 10 stitches, bind off center 10 stitches, knit across last 10 stitches.

Work across these last 10 stitches for six rows. K2tog at the neck edge every other row.

Work until front is the same length as the back.

Bind off.

Pick up yarn on the other side and repeat.

Bind off all stitches.

Sleeves (make two):

Cast on 20.

Work 8 rows of stockinette stitches.

On next row, increase one stitch at each edge.

Continue, increasing two stitches after every fourth row, until sleeve measures 3¹/₂".

Bind off all stitches.

To Assemble:

Sew shoulder seams together. Match sleeves to shoulder and sew on. Sew side seams together.

Neck:

Pick up and knit 16 stitches along front of sweater, 2 at shoulder, 14 along the back and 2 more at the other shoulder. (Note: since teddies have small necks, it may be simpler to work the neck on double-pointed needles.) If working in the round, knit four rows. If working back and forth on straight needles, knit 1 row, purl 1 row. Repeat these two rows one more time.

Turn the page for an exciting sneak preview
of what's coming in April from Harlequin NEXT!
RASPBERRY SHERBET KISSES
by Ellyn Bache

Okay. The beginning. The day Jeremy Taylor and I broke up. An event that still makes me so mad I can almost forget my handcuffs.

I was twenty-three. Practically a baby. In *love*. I had picked Jeremy up from work because his car was in the shop, and the first thing he did was turn the radio to that loud rock station he liked, where the music was so thick it always made me see an oatmeal-gray mush in front of my eyes.

"Didn't you ever hear the rule saying the driver gets to decide what to listen to?" I asked, trying to sound flirty instead of irritated.

"Oh, honey," he crooned, running a finger over the side of my face with a lightness that was more tease than touch. Goose bumps shivered all up and down my arms, and I forgot the radio entirely. I couldn't help it. Call it hormones, immaturity, stupidity; in any case, being close to Jeremy about took my breath away. I concentrated on the road and tried not to notice his strong, square jaw out of the corner of my eye. Or the blacker-than-black stubble on his cheek, which

I thought was the most masculine facial feature I'd ever laid eyes on. Or the dimples that softened his expression every time he smiled or spoke. I was a fool for Jeremy's dimples.

The oatmeal-mush music throbbed on for a while. Then suddenly the Emergency Broadcast System tone came on, and as always happens when I hear that high, whining sound, everything in front of me turned such a bright orange that the road was barely visible. "Shut that off!" I yelled. "I can hardly see!"

Jeremy switched off the radio. He stared at me hard until I turned to face him. His dimples flattened into a disapproving pout. "What does the Emergency Broadcast System have to do with what you can see, LilyRose? When you say things like that, you sound half-crazy."

Half-crazy! I was about to blurt something sharp and snippy when the Sheffield vow of silence cut me off, slicing through my brain in the oft-repeated words of my mother, Zee: "Say something even once, and it's out there forever, honey. You can't unsay it. Can't control it. All it can do is hurt you."

Believe me, I knew. But under the pressure of Jeremy's less-than-loving gaze, it also occurred to me that after four months of serious dating, and especially after the discussion we'd almost-but-not-quite had about where our relationship was going, the man had a right to some information. "I've got something to show you," I told him. "Something I want to show you right now. It's at Mama's."

Jeremy groaned. Ignoring him, I made a U-turn and headed for Cardinal Circle.

The house where I grew up and where Mama still lives is a big, rambling, old-fashioned place with a swing on the front porch and a backyard that in those days was full of Daddy's flower beds. Inside, there's no central air, just window air conditioners in some of the rooms and ceiling fans in the rest. I knocked once and then yoo-hooed for Mama as I led Jeremy through the open front screen and down the hall to the kitchen, where Mama was making herself a salad for dinner. Daddy was gone until the end of the week—he was an independent trucker who owned his own rig and hauled the loads himself.

Mama stopped slicing tomatoes and looked up with a quizzical expression, focusing first on me and then on Jeremy and back again. "Well," she said. "What brings you two here? Let me get you some nice cold tea."

I held up my hand to stop her. "Mama, I've decided to show Jeremy those magazine articles." I adopted my best professional tone, which in those days was anything but convincing.

If Mama had her doubts, she didn't voice them. She raised her eyebrows, set down the slicing knife and without a word went out to get her file of clippings about synesthesia.

Synesthesia. I hated the fact that it sounded like a disease. It isn't a sickness. Synesthesia means having two or more senses linked—your vision linked with your hearing, say, so that every time you hear the Emergency Broadcast System tone, you see the world through an overlay of orange. Some of the articles said synesthesia affected one percent of the population, most of them women. Some said one person in every two thousand. In any case, not very many. No wonder people didn't know about it. I told myself not to blame Jeremy just yet for saying I was half-crazy. He'd change his mind once he finished reading the articles Mama set out on the dining-room table. He'd apologize in his most penitent tone, all dimples and remorse.

I had been eleven or twelve before Mama found that first write-up about synesthesia in one of her women's magazines. Until then Mama and Daddy and I were as ignorant as everyone else in not even knowing it had a name. What we did know was that I saw glass columns when I tasted mint, and golden spheres whenever old Mrs. Leona Richie sang *The Star Spangled Banner* at a ball game or public meeting. Those things had been happening for so long that none of us thought it was unusual, but even so, it was nice to find out I wasn't the only one.

Much as we liked synesthesia having a name, Daddy hated as much as I did the fact that it sounded so ominous. "Sinas *what*? Sin-ess *thee* zee-ah?" He would act as if he couldn't pronounce it at all, then snap his fingers and say, "Oh, *now* I know what you're saying. *Sinus*. You're talking about LilyRose's *sinus* problems."

He became an expert at joking in this way, and sometimes it was a good thing. For example, Mama's roast beef usually made me see the kind of tan-and-white marble arches I'd seen in movies about fancy villas in far-off countries, but not if it didn't taste just right. Once, when she served an over-cooked roast to company, I blurted out in front of everyone, "Why, Mama! The arches in this meat are all flattened out!" Daddy laughed before anyone could even register shock, and said with a chuckle, "Oh, there goes LilyRose's sinus problem acting up again." He sounded so casual that no one ever thought to question how a roast could have arches or what that had to do with sinuses. They just assumed that impaired drainage must affect a person's sense of taste more than they knew. This kind of incident happened all the time.

Then the day arrived when Mama's article collection became our weapon in the war against my reputation. I think all along we'd known it would come to this. Without Mama's arsenal of clippings, I might have ended up in jail long before the ripe age of thirty-five.

The best things in life are free

Kate Bishop needs money and fast.
Her roof needs replacing. Her kids need
tuition and her ex-husband is a cheap creep.
Then her wildest fantasy comes true—
she wins the lottery. Suddenly, everything
changes. Her wish came true, but now what?

Wish Come True

USA TODAY bestselling author

Patricia Kay

Romantic
SUSPENSE

**Excitement, danger
and passion guaranteed!**

USA TODAY bestselling author
Marie Ferrarella
is back with the second installment
in her popular miniseries,
*The Doctors Pulaski: Medicine
just got more interesting...*
DIAGNOSIS: DANGER is on sale
April 2007 from Silhouette®
Romantic Suspense (formerly
Silhouette Intimate Moments).

*Look for it wherever
you buy books!*

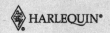

Every great love has a story to tell™

**If you're a romantic at heart,
you'll definitely want to read
this new series.**

Available April 24

The Marriage Bed by Judith Arnold

An emotional story about a couple's love that
is put to the test when the shocking truth of
a long-buried secret comes to the surface.

&

Family Stories by Tessa McDermid

A couple's epic love story is pieced together
by their granddaughter in time for their
seventy-fifth anniversary.

And look for

The Scrapbook by Lynnette Kent

&

When Love Is True by Joan Kilby

from Harlequin® Everlasting Love™ this June.

Pick up a book today!

www.eHarlequin.com   HELMAY07

REQUEST YOUR FREE BOOKS!

2 FREE NOVELS PLUS 2 FREE GIFTS!

Ne**xt**™

There's the life you planned. And there's what comes next.

YES! Please send me 2 FREE Harlequin® NEXT™ novels and my 2 FREE mystery gifts. After receiving them, if I don't wish to receive any more books, I can return the shipping statement marked "cancel." If I don't cancel, I will receive 4 brand-new novels every other month and be billed just $3.99 per book in the U.S. or $4.74 per book in Canada, plus 25¢ shipping and handling per book plus applicable taxes, if any.* That's a savings of over 25% off the cover price! I understand that accepting the 2 free books and gifts places me under no obligation to buy anything. I can always return a shipment and cancel at any time. Even if I never buy anything from Harlequin, the two free books and gifts are mine to keep forever.   155 HDN EL33 355 HDN EL4F

Name	(PLEASE PRINT)	

Address		Apt. #

City	State/Prov.	Zip/Postal Code

Signature (if under 18, a parent or guardian must sign)

Order online at www.TryNEXTNovels.com

Or mail to the **Harlequin Reader Service®**:

IN U.S.A.: P.O. Box 1867, Buffalo, NY 14240-1867
IN CANADA: P.O. Box 609, Fort Erie, Ontario L2A 5X3

Not valid to current Harlequin NEXT subscribers.

Want to try two free books from another line?
Call 1-800-873-8635 or visit www.morefreebooks.com

* Terms and prices subject to change without notice. NY residents add applicable sales tax. Canadian residents will be charged applicable provincial taxes and GST. This offer is limited to one order per household. All orders subject to approval. Credit or debit balances in a customer's account(s) may be offset by any other outstanding balance owed by or to the customer. Please allow 4 to 6 weeks for delivery.

Your Privacy: Harlequin Books is committed to protecting your privacy. Our Privacy Policy is available online at www.eHarlequin.com or upon request from the Harlequin Reader Service. From time to time we make our lists of customers available to reputable firms who may have a product or service of interest to you. If you would prefer we not share your name and address, please check here. ☐

NEXT07R

HARLEQUIN Romance

presents a brand-new trilogy by

PATRICIA THAYER

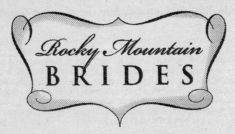

Rocky Mountain
BRIDES

Three sisters come home to wed.

In April don't miss

Raising the Rancher's Family,

followed by

The Sheriff's Pregnant Wife,

on sale May 2007,

and

A Mother for the Tycoon's Child,

on sale June 2007.